SUN
THIEF

Also by Jamie Buxton

Temple Boys

SUN THIEF

JAMIE BUXTON

EGMONT

EGMONT

We bring stories to life

First published in Great Britain in 2015 by Egmont UK Limited
The Yellow Building, 1 Nicholas Road, London W11 4AN

Text copyright © 2015 Jamie Buxton

The moral rights of the author have been asserted

ISBN 978 1 4052 67991

55467/1

www.egmont.co.uk

A CIP catalogue record for this title is available from the British
Library

Typeset by Avon DataSet Ltd, Bidford on Avon, Warwickshire
Printed and bound in Great Britain by the CPI Group

For Amanda.
Thank you.

1. In which I tell you pretty much all I've learned before we've even started

1. Don't lie.
2. Don't kill.
3. Don't steal.
4. Don't marry more than one person at a time.
5. Be happy with what you've got.
6. Be kind to your parents so long as they are kind to you. If not, don't bother.
7. Take a day off when you need to.
8. Choose your god then stick to it.
9. Don't make models of him/her. It only leads to trouble.
10. Now think of something yourself, you lazy dog.

2. In which you have the huge honour of meeting me

So here I am, standing on top of a pyramid. I'm as high as the sky and king of the world.

In front of me, the Great River is a big, fat, dark, lazy snake, winding through a patchwork of fields: green grass, golden wheat, black earth.

Behind me, the desert is as dull as a dead lion's hide.

1

On my left and far, far away, the setting sun has just turned the stones of the old city to gold.

On my right, our town is a muddle of narrow streets and four-square, flat-roofed houses built of brown mud brick. Fires blink like bright eyes as people cook their evening meal. On the back road that leads in from the north, I can just see a small dust cloud. It's tearing along at a fair old lick and there's a dark man-shape in the middle of it, like the grit in a ball of raw cotton.

When you're up on a pyramid, you're standing on an old king who's buried somewhere in the pile of rocks beneath you. Soldiers used to march around its base to keep rabble like me away and the common people had to crawl up a long stone causeway to ask for blessings from the priests who prayed in his temple. But the new king in the south has banned the old gods and told us to worship the sun. The Aten, he's called. I suppose the king has his reasons, but I can't help feeling it's a bit boring. I mean, what does this Aten do except shine? The old gods got up to all kinds of mischief, some of which is too shocking to talk about, but that makes me like them more.

Still, look on the bright side: no gods means no priests; no priests means no guards; no guards means I get to climb the Great Pyramid whenever I feel like it.

So I'm up in the sky and feeling great when I suddenly realise that the little cloud of dust I saw on the back road could be a guest coming to the inn. And if it is, I have to

be back there to meet him or I'm in trouble – a muddy
great heap of it.

3. In which a guest actually arrives at the inn

As it happens, I reach the inn just before my parents return
from visiting neighbours, and they get back just before the
guest bangs at the courtyard gate.

I'm sticky with sweat as I open it, still breathing heavily
from running home. I grazed my knee from sliding down
the pyramid too fast and the sticky trickle of blood is a
cool itch on my skin.

The new guest is a big mud-coloured man with thick
arms like rolls of linen and a face as smooth as wet clay.
Dust is sticking to his shaven head and he doesn't greet us
and he doesn't say any of the usual things.

Not: 'I was wondering if you had a room, and do you
serve meals?' (Regular guest.)

Not: 'I say, what a charming inn! Now, would you be
so good as to furnish me with a room for a week or so?
And is that cooking I smell? How delicious.' (Will try and
leave without paying his bill.)

Not: 'Gods, what a dump. Still, I suppose it's the only
place I'll find in this miserable town.' (Will pay, but argue
every penny.)

3

Not: 'I'm a poor, hungry traveller and I need a place to rest my head.' (Has money, but pretends he hasn't.)

This man says: 'I want good stew, strong beer and a quiet room.' And stares through my father into the space behind him. There's something in the way he talks, the way he uses just the right amount of words and no more, that feels menacing. I don't know why. I'm ready for my father to shake his head and say: 'Sorry – no rooms for tonight,' but I guess three things stop him.

1. My mother starts to make cooing, welcoming noises. She's fiddling with her good wig – the one with the beads woven into the braids that she stole from her mother's hoard of grave goods, though she will never admit it.

2. Although anyone can see that this new guest is trouble, something about him makes it hard to say no.

3. (the clincher) My parents are in no position to refuse anyone, even if they think he's a murderer. Even if they think he's a mass murderer, for that matter.

You see, ever since the new king banned the old gods, and the plague started devastating the Two Kingdoms, business has more or less dried up. The tourists who used to come to the pyramids and leave offerings at the temples are staying away and the little shrine at the back of our inn is deserted. Worse than that, no one really knows if the old ways of doing things are legal and, as a result, our regular drinkers – tomb builders, wall painters, grave-goods

4

makers, professional mourners and the like – are broke.

But the new guest doesn't look like the kind of man to worry about things like that. After he's eaten his stew and drunk his beer, he quietly says he's going to the shrine and no one will disturb him while he's there.

Not: 'I don't want to be disturbed.' Not: 'No one should disturb me.' Just: 'I will not be disturbed,' like he knows that if he says it, it won't happen.

We all sit around feeling slightly stunned. A few people wander in for a drink or a chat. I serve two travelling carpenters looking for work and a thickset man with a broken nose who wants to know if we've got a room, but he bets we're too busy for the likes of him.

'Only one guest and there he is,' I say, nodding to the new man. He's just left the shrine and is sitting on a bench the other side of the courtyard, leaning back against the wall, his eyes closed against the glare of the setting sun.

I guess the thickset man doesn't like the look of him any more than the carpenters because they all drink up and leave.

I, on the other hand, have to serve him.

'More beer, boy.'

Like I said, he uses exactly the right amount of words – no more, no less – and when he finally opens his eyes and finds me staring at him, he gives me a slow, mean, crocodile stare that zings straight into my brain. It isn't nice at all, but the funny thing is that the meaner he looks, the more I want him to notice me, even though it frightens me half to death.

4. In which I talk about mud (yes, mud)

Next morning, first light of day, and my mother is screaming questions at me. I don't answer because she's managing to do that herself:

'What have you been doing? I tell you what you've been doing – playing with mud. What have you done to earn your keep? Nothing. What have we done to deserve you? Nothing. We've worked our fingers to the bone for you and what do we get in return? Nothing, boy. Nothing.'

And however hard I try, however much I hope, nothing is exactly what I mean to them. They found me in the Great River, you see, when I was a baby and although I call my father 'father' and my mother 'mother', I don't think they'll ever think of me as their son, although things might have been different if they hadn't had Imi, their daughter, a few years later. But it's no use worrying, because suppose they'd had Imi *before* they found me? They'd have left me for the crocodiles, I reckon. After a bad day, sometimes I wish they had, but then, after a good one, I'm glad they didn't, so I suppose you could say it all balances out.

'Yes, mother,' I say, but she doesn't so much as glance at me. All the time she's been yelling at me, she's had one eye on our new guest, whom she's started calling the Quiet Gentleman. He's sitting on the bench in the sun and looking at her through narrowed eyes. I notice that she's still wearing her best dress and her dead mother's wig, and she's painted her eyes with thick lines of kohl.

So I sweep the yard, I repair the gate, I fix a hole in the roof, I mend a bench, I fetch, I carry, and then when I'm knackered, my mother clips me on the side of the head, accuses me of slacking and orders me to make more plates and beakers.

So I do that too.

My pottery area is in the corner of the yard close to the kitchen and across from the Quiet Gentleman. No bit of him moves apart from his eyelids, which have closed again.

I begin to work. First, I lift the cloth off the special mud I use, feel its consistency, add a touch more water and knead it. Next, I put the mud in the middle of my potter's wheel and give the wheel a spin. Then I begin to work it.

I'm good at this. In my hands, a blob of mud flattens and stretches to make a saucer, a plate or a cup. I lose myself in my work, as I always do, and suddenly there's a row of plates and a tray of beakers drying in the sun. Twenty plates and forty beakers.

Each plate will last for one meal and the beakers for an evening. Back before the business fell off, I had to make twenty plates a day. Now the same number will last a month.

'Boy,' the Quiet Gentleman says, his eyes still closed. 'Mud boy. What else can you do with that stuff?'

He's talking so quietly that I have to strain to hear him.

'Make animals,' I say, 'as a matter of fact.'

'Like this, as a matter of fact?'

He holds up a lion that I must have left out.

'Yes,' I answer.

'Any others?' he asks.

'Falcons,' I say. 'And lionesses and dogs and cobras.'

'And storks?' he asked. 'And a sphinx or two. Maybe a crocodile?'

'Maybe,' I answer, wondering what he's after.

A pause. His eyes snap open. 'You will show me,' he says. 'Mud boy.' And then they shut again.

Mud boy. Not a bad name. I am a mud boy. In my humble opinion, but in no one else's, this makes me special. Yes, indeed. For the People of the Two Kingdoms, the People of the Great River, the People of the Black Earth, us in other words, mud is life.

Why are we the greatest nation on earth? Mud.

What do our crops grow in? The Great River's mud.

How do we build our houses? You guessed it: from bricks made of mud.

8

What's wrong with the desert? Extreme lack of mud.

If you work in an inn, you soon see how like mud we all are. Give us too much to drink and we collapse like wet mud. Give us too little to drink and we crack like dry mud. In life, we start out firm and strong and smooth like newly mixed-up mud and then, in the end, we just crumble away like old mud.

But here's an interesting thought. I know the new king has banned the old gods, but that doesn't mean they've gone away, does it? No, they're hiding and I know where.

You see, the old woman who used to sweep our yard told me that in the early days of the world, Ra and Isis and Osiris got bored strolling around the muddy young world on their own, so they decided to use the mud to make the man and the woman, the dog and the cat, the crocodile and the hippo, the horse and the cow, and every other animal you can think of. In other words, they must know a thing or two about mud, and that's a clue.

Here's another. As she swept our yard, the old woman used to mutter a rhyme as she worked.

The wheel turns, the wheel burns
The stork and the falcon fly.
The wheel turns, the wheel burns
The cobra and lioness cry.

The wheel turns, the wheel burns
The sphinx is buried in earth.
The wheel turns, the wheel burns
The queen of the sun dies of thirst.

The wheel turns, the wheel burns
The king in the cavern turns green.
The wheel turns, the wheel burns
The ram and the phoenix grow lean.

So hey for the wind and hey for the air
For they don't care for the wheel,
And the black dog walks and the black dog stalks
And the ghosts of the dead city squeal.

And the wheel turns and the wheel burns
The ghouls in the graveyard sigh,
The wheel turns and the wheel burns
And the stork and falcon fly . . .

And so on. And so on. And so on. That old song is as much a part of my world as the feel of dust under my feet or the smell of woodsmoke in the evening, but I never really thought about it as I followed the old woman around the yard.

Then just last year, after the new king had declared the Aten to be the one true god and his soldiers had closed the temples, the old woman checked we were alone, put her broom down, grabbed me by the arm and marched me to the empty temple at the foot of the Great Pyramid. I was frightened of the enormous stone gateway, the dark doors and the huge statues of dead gods and dead kings, their faces and names hacked off on the orders of the new king.

On we walked, through empty courtyards and dusty, high-pillared halls. Courtyards and halls grew smaller, then darker, then even darker and smaller but the more scared I grew, the harder the old woman's nails dug into my arm.

At last we paused at a low, square doorway. Inside I could hear scrabbling and snarling. The old woman pushed me to one side and threw stones through the dark doorway until a wild dog rushed out and past us. Then she led me in.

We waited in the dark stillness. Slowly my eyes adjusted and dim shapes began to emerge from the walls. Figures carved into stone. The king's soldiers had been at work with their chisels here as well and it was hard to make the shapes out until the old woman took my hand, laid it on the stone and started to chant.

Through the stone, under the roughness of the chisel marks, the shapes of the falcon and the stork, the sphinx and the lioness pressed up against my fingers. Gods and goddesses.

'The new king thinks he killed 'em, but he's just driven

'em out of the stone,' the old woman whispered in my ear. 'They're hiding now. Boy of water, boy of earth: you'll find 'em, boy. You'll bring 'em back. That's your job.'

At the time what she said made no sense to me, but when you're young nothing does.

All I know is that if I mix water and earth it makes mud, and in the mud I can find the stork, the falcon, the cobra, the lioness and all the rest of them. It's not me that's doing it; the shapes of the animals press up against my fingers from inside the mud. The gods are in the animals and the animals are in the mud and that is where they're hiding.

5. In which I introduce you to our dead neighbours

No time to think about that now. Here comes my mother, swooping down on me, her head pecking the air like a chicken.

'Time for you to stop daydreaming and fetch your little sister. Can't you see how late it is? What are you thinking?'

She glances at the Quiet Gentleman out of the corner of her eye and simpers: 'What is it with the young of today? They're like chalk and cheese, him and my daughter. She's as good as gold, but he's –' and her voice takes on an all too familiar rasp '– he's like a moonstruck cow. A burden ever since we took him in. Go, child. And be back before sunset or there'll be a clip round the ear waiting for you.'

She points up at the sun, which is where it always is at this time of day, and nips my earlobe between her finger and thumb. What I'm thinking is that I was told to fetch my sister from her aunt's house tomorrow morning, but someone's changed their mind and forgot to let me know.

'But it's too late,' I protest. 'I'll never be able to get there and back in time.'

'Then hurry! And don't go taking any short cuts through *you know where*.'

'But . . .'

'GO!'

Imi, Imi, Imi. My little sister. My parents' daughter, their real child, as they never stop reminding me. I'm big enough to admit that Imi's great, even if she is my kid sister. But sometimes, *sometimes*, I think that if she wasn't so perfect, I might seem a little less bad.

I scrape the mud off my potter's wheel, prop it against the wall and leave.

The aunt doesn't live far away, just the other side of the pyramids, but between our home and hers is *you know where* – a place that scares the loincloth off me.

It's like a town, this place. It has streets. It has squares. It has houses, and the rich stay in the big ones and the poor stay in the small ones. But there's one VERY BIG

13

difference between this town and the one I live in: everyone in it is dead.

I know, I know. Dying is not really dying. This life is a preparation for the next one which is far, far better and you go there surrounded by all your favourite possessions and pets and food and drink and blah blah blah . . .

But here's the catch. To keep your spirit alive, your relatives have to say your name and bring food to your tomb, and just to check, your spirit flies back from the underworld like a bird every evening. The houses of the dead sometimes even have a little perch above the front door for the soul to rest on.

But what happens to souls that have been forgotten, whose relatives don't turn up with biscuits and milk? I'll tell you. They become wandering ghouls. Not just hungry ghosts but hungry, *angry* ghosts.

Now, because I actually have eyes in my head and a tiny little bit of reasoning power, I know for A FACT that grieving relatives have pretty much given up visiting these houses of the dead. Result? An AWFUL LOT of whispering ghouls and MORE and MORE every day.

Here I am, walking past the wall that surrounds the City of the Dead. Now I'm passing its main gate and I look in – and wish I hadn't. The houses of the dead are spilling darkness. It fills the streets and alleyways and in the darkness are the ghouls.

My friends, it's a good place to avoid.

6. In which my sister is too neighbourly

The aunt is rich. She has a two-roomed house with a bread oven out the back and a slave who does just about everything for her. My little sister Imi goes there to learn manners, weaving, hair-braiding – all a girl needs to hook a good husband.

When I get to the house, Imi's hair is neatly braided and she's showing off a new tunic and a brightly coloured belt. She jumps up when she sees me and throws her arms around me. I give her a little ram I made earlier and she runs into the house to say goodbye and thank you to her aunt.

Who comes out into the street in order to be rude to me.

'Oh, it's you, is it?' she says.

'Of course it's him,' Imi says. 'Who else would it be?' She doesn't say it sarcastically. She doesn't understand sarcasm.

'Never you mind. He's late.'

I open my mouth to protest, but decide it's not worth it.

'Look, he brought me a sheep!' Imi holds up the little ram. The aunt snatches it and holds it out at arm's length, squinting the way old people do.

'Blasphemy,' she says. 'I should grind it to dust. The

Aten is the one true god and the blessed one has eaten all the old gods.'

'So if he's eaten them, how could this be a god?' I ask innocently. 'It's just an animal.'

The aunt looks at me suspiciously, but hands the clay model back to Imi.

'Right, Imi, time to head off,' I say.

Please note, the aunt has not asked me if I want a drink of cool, refreshing water or a place to rest before setting out on the long journey home.

'You'll have to hurry if you want to get back before dark,' is all she says.

'Yes, Aunt.'

She hates it when I call her aunt. Auntauntauntauntaunt.

'And don't just stand there gawping.'

'Yes, Aunt.'

'Off you go then.'

'Yes, Auntie.'

'What did you call me?'

'Auntie, Aunt.' I get the scowl I was waiting for and off we go. Imi is skipping along and holding a bunch of weeds that she manages to make look like a posy of flowers. I'm walking quickly because I don't want to be seen running after my little sister, but don't want her to get too far ahead either. And everything's fine until we get to the City of the Dead. Then Imi stops right at the gate and looks through it.

'Come on,' I say, walking past very deliberately. 'It's getting late.'

It's true. The sun's already disappearing behind the pyramids and bats are fluttering between the houses of the dead, black scraps patted by an invisible wind.

'Let's go that way.' Imi points down the street that leads straight into the heart of the shadowy city. 'It's much faster. You go down there and turn left and then there's a hole in the wall and you're home.'

'It may be quicker, but it's too.dangerous,' I say. 'We'll get lost and then we won't get home at all. And you know you're not allowed.'

'It's not dark yet,' Imi says, holding the ram up so he's pointing in the direction she wants to go.

'It will be soon.'

'Are you scared?' she asks.

She's not teasing me, I know, but it still niggles. 'NO!' I snap.

'Silly. Come on!'

'I'm not . . . no, IMI! COME BACK!'

Because she's running through the gate and straight into the City of the Dead.

I make a sound that's a cross between a shout and a whisper. Make too much noise and the ghouls will hear.

She disappears between two buildings. I can hear the *pat-pat-pat* of her feet. Fine dust hanging in the air is the only sign of her.

'*IMI!*'

I take a step, then another down the long straight street and try to look straight ahead. My footsteps *paff-paff* through the dust, beating out the words: *angry, hungry ghouls; angry, hungry ghouls.* Outside the houses are the dried-up remains of meals left for the dead: empty bowls, sheaves of grain, the odd goose bone . . . Some of the doors have crumbled or been kicked in and even though I don't want to look, I can see long pale shapes in the darkness.

Mummies.

My heart starts whacking away inside me like it wants to escape and my stomach's chasing it up my throat. I reach the place where Imi turned off the main street. It's an alley between buildings so narrow I have to turn sideways to fit. Another lane crosses it in a T.

Left or right? I think I hear the patter of Imi's sandals and follow the sound, but the alley jinks around a corner and stops dead at a sagging wall. I want to howl with despair.

'*IMI*. This isn't a joke!' I do the shouty whisper again and look up. The sky's darker now and I can see stars behind the pyramids rising above the rooftops. I jump as something flaps off into the air. Too big for a bat. An owl. It must be an owl.

Imi, I hate you!

I backtrack and take the first turning in the direction of

home. It's another alleyway, very dark and narrow, but the gloom seems to lessen in the distance. Perhaps I'm nearly on the other side. But when I get there I stop dead. I could not be more wrong. Instead of heading out of the City of the Dead, I've been going right into the middle of it.

I'm looking down a wide, straight street lined with the grandest buildings I have ever seen. They're built of stone with pillars and porches. The walls inside the porches are painted. I can just make out a man fishing, a woman being waited on by dancing girls. The relatives of the rich dead folk didn't just leave meals, they left feasts: piles of grain, pitchers of beer, jars of wine – all dry, all dust, all pecked by birds and gnawed by dogs. Under the blown sand, I feel smooth flagstones beneath my feet.

Ahead of me the pyramids loom above the rooftops. They've never seemed so big and black and jagged. The ghouls are gathering – I know they are – and I can't see Imi anywhere.

My steps slow. I am awed by the grandeur of everything around me. I'm sure I can hear dark things calling me in whispers. Dread seeps through cracked walls. I stare into a doorway under a wide porch and am backing away from it when something clutches my ankle . . .

I stumble and fall backwards, too shocked to make a sound. A hand flutters over my mouth. I screw my eyes shut, feel breath on my face . . .

'*Sssss!*' the ghoul hisses. '*Shhh.*'

Then: 'Open your eyes. It's me!'

I open my eyes. Yes, it's Imi, but she looks terrified.

'Shh! People. Here!'

When you're well-behaved like Imi, getting caught is unimaginably bad – even worse than ghosts – but I'm so relieved to see her that I stop being scared for a moment. Her beautiful new tunic, once so white it glowed, is filthy now, but I don't care.

Then I hear the voices too. They're coming from both ends of the street so we're trapped. Some families hire guards to watch over the graves. If it's them, we're in trouble. I look for places to hide. The porches are wide open to the street. It'll have to be inside one of the houses of the dead.

The nearest door is twice my height and set with copper panels. It scrapes open just enough for us to slip in. Half the roof has fallen in so I can just make out a broken chair, a bed, furniture, musical instruments, smashed jars. There are shelves all the way round stacked with mummies – people on the left, cats and other animals on the right. They're lying this way and that, like there's been an earthquake, and the floor is crunchy with shattered tiles. The air is musty and musky.

Imi starts to whimper. 'I don't like it, I don't like it.'

I almost snap, IT'S YOUR FAULT, but control myself.

The voices outside are getting closer. Greetings are

called. I lift Imi on to a shelf, clear a space, then slide her behind a family of mummified cats.

They're right outside now. I dive behind a mummy lying on the bottom shelf, but it's so light it falls to the floor. Something quick and dark scrabbles away.

'What was that?' A startled voice comes from right outside the door. There's no time to pull the mummy back on to the shelf, so I roll off and pull it on top of me. It's big enough to hide me, but I'm breathing in mummy scent and mummy dust. I'm breathing in . . . someone dead.

'It came from in there.' A second voice, cold and sneering.

They heard me. They're coming in.

7. In which I overhear what I wish I hadn't

I hear a third voice: 'What? In here?' I think I've heard it before, but I can't quite remember when. It sounds slow and rather stupid.

Three voices then: one cold and sneery, one worried and jittery, and one slow and stupid.

'What do you think it is?' Worried and Jittery asks.

'Only one way to find out,' Cold and Sneery answers.

'What?' Slow and Stupid joins in.

'Go and look,' Cold and Sneery snaps.

'Why is it always me?' Slow and Stupid grumbles.

Where have I heard him before?

'Because you're so brave,' Cold and Sneery sneers coldly.

The door scrapes across the floor. I hope and hope and hope it's too dark for them to see our footprints in the dust.

'Anything?' Worried and Jittery sounds, well, worried and jittery.

'Can't see,' Slow and Stupid says. 'It's dark and I don't like it. It's full of . . .'

'You're not scared, are you?' Cold and Sneery interrupts. 'Just get a move on.'

Footsteps shuffle across the floor. Something skitters away in the darkness. Slow and Stupid shrieks out a sound like WHUFFLE! which brings the others running. I pull my mummy as close to me as possible and then it starts to move, with a scraping and a scratching, as if the body inside is trying to get out.

A scream gathers in my chest.

'What?' says Worried and Jittery. 'What's going on?'

'Something's moving. It ran across the floor!'

'It's just a rat! Come out, you idiot!' Cold and Sneery laughs.

The mummy shifts. Squeaks. Then I realise it's not a dead person trying to get out of the mummy, it's rats – a disturbed family of rats. I feel around until I find the rat hole. The last thing I want is baby rats crawling out all over me and the first thing I want is for those men to go away.

But they stay. Of course they stay. They go back outside, stand under the big covered porch, and they start to talk.

Cold and Sneery starts off with, 'Well? I told you it was a good place to meet in secret. I'd have thought you were used to tombs by now.'

'Not with bodies in, I'm not,' Slow and Stupid says. 'Not like Jatty.'

'Oh, I forgot. You just dig the tombs and leave the hard work to everyone else. And don't use names, you idiot,' Cold and Sneery says.

'It's hard work digging tombs,' Slow and Stupid says.

'Not as hard as breaking in and finding out that they haven't mummified the body properly and the first thing you touch is an oozing grave shroud,' Worried and Jittery answers.

'Enough with the hard-luck stories,' Cold and Sneery says. 'What have you got to report?'

'We think we've found him,' Worried and Jittery answers, talking fast. 'He's staying nearby. Bek's description matches: big, ugly, moon-faced, scary bloke. Keeps himself to himself.'

'What did I say about names? Oh, never mind. Where exactly is he staying?'

I've got a pain starting in the arm that's trapped under

my body and I think the baby rats have found the hand that's blocking the hole in the mummy's side because I can feel their warm noses and itchy whiskers against it. But when I hear the answer, I forget all discomfort.

'An inn. This side of town. Got an old shrine round the back.'

'And you've checked this out?'

'I did,' says Slow and Stupid. 'He came into town by the north road and I followed him. Had a drink at the inn and took a room.'

'You did?'

'No, he did. Think I'm stupid?'

'Yes. Did he recognise you?'

'No. I saw him on a job years ago. He never noticed me then and he didn't notice me now.'

I remember where I heard the voice before. He was one of the men at the inn yesterday. Without a doubt, the Quiet Gentleman is the ugly, moon-faced, scary bloke.

The man with the cold voice is talking again, sounding excited. 'That double-crossing rat. The first thing we have to do is search his room. He won't have got rid of it. Trust me. And if he's hidden it we can make him talk. No, I've got a better idea. We'll wait and see whether he's moving on or staying put, and then we'll . . .'

At last they start walking away and their voices grow fainter before they fade to nothing.

I push the mummy off me and stand up. It's darker

outside now and almost pitch-black inside. I can't see the shelf Imi's on and whichever way I turn it's just going to be mummies everywhere.

'Imi,' I whisper. 'Imi.'

No answer. I force myself to think. The door must be ahead of me so Imi's to my left. I feel for the shelf I left her on, scattering mummified cats and birds and not caring how many rat families I'm disturbing. My fingers touch something warm.

'Imi?' I whisper again.

'Yes?'

'You all right?'

'I was asleep. The cats were trying to talk to me, but I couldn't understand what they were saying because they were talking cat language.' I feel her sit up. 'Can we go home now?'

That's Imi – instead of being frightened by cat ghosts, she talks to them. I almost hug her.

Outside, the pyramids bite black-toothed chunks from a bright field of stars.

The wheel turns, the wheel burns . . . The old woman told me the rhyme was all about the gods as they go wheeling across the sky. I can see the sphinx up there, and the ram, and think about the great boat below the horizon that carries the sun across the underworld sea so it rises fresh and new in the morning.

Fresh and new.

It would be good to feel fresh and new and hopeful and not scared, but I'm not stupid. I know who those men were: tomb robbers, the worst criminals in the world. Ruthless, violent and secretive. They'll kill anyone who knows who they are, and from what they were saying, it sounds like the Quiet Gentleman is one too. And if that's not enough to worry about . . .

8. In which help comes from an unlikely source and I behave oddly

. . . I'm in trouble.

How much? Quick answer: a heap. Long answer: trouble, trouble with more trouble piled on top and then doubled. Double, double, double trouble. And my mother doesn't care who knows about it.

She shouts at me so loudly as I walk into the courtyard, with Imi holding tightly on to my hand, that it's a wonder the walls don't fall down. We're late. It's dark. Anything could have happened. We could have been attacked by robbers, by wild dogs, by lions. And look at the state of Imi: what did I do? Did I try to kill her out of black-hearted jealousy?

It's a rare busy night and all the drinkers at the inn are

nudging each other and shaking their heads, and in case you're wondering why I don't run off and hide, my father is gripping my arm so tightly he leaves a bracelet of bruises around it.

And there's nothing I can say. We got lost in the City of the Dead, the one place I was forbidden to enter? We were trapped there by tomb robbers? That just means more danger for Imi and more trouble for me.

A couple of my father's cronies start to mutter about bad blood and how I need a good thrashing, when the Quiet Gentleman, who's been sitting on his own on his usual bench, stands up.

'You've said enough,' he tells my mother, who shuts up like she's lost the power of speech.

'And why don't you let go of the boy's arm?' This to my father, who obeys.

'And why don't you step back?' This to my father's cronies.

'There,' the Quiet Gentleman says, 'that's better for everyone. And now we ask the little girl what happened.' His smile reminds me of a split in an overripe melon.

This is where we get to the bit where you understand why I actually like my sister.

'I ran away from him,' Imi says, looking up at the Quiet Gentleman. 'And I got lost and then I was scared, but he came looking for me and found me and he rescued me from the ghosts and brought me home.'

Perfect answer.

The Quiet Gentleman looks around. As well as the drinkers, a small crowd has gathered at the gate, attracted by my mother's screeching. He says: 'All these people want to buy a drink. You'd better get busy, boy.'

I get busy and my parents sell more beer and wine than they have since the shrine became illegal, and I get more tips than I've had in my life and a few slaps on the back for being a good boy.

But I don't tell the Quiet Gentleman about the men who were talking about him in the City of the Dead. I don't try to warn him. Why? Because if I tell him what I overheard it'll be like pointing a finger at him and saying *tomb robber*.

And then he'll have to kill me.

Next morning I get up early, fetch water, sweep the courtyard, then buy fresh bread and goat's milk for breakfast.

By the time I'm back, the Quiet Gentleman is sitting in his usual place on the bench. The morning sun's not too hot and he's closed his eyes and tilted up his head towards it. He's found one of my mud animals – a sphinx – and he's holding it up to the sun as well.

As soon as he hears me, his eyes open sleepily. Whatever I do, wherever I go, he watches me like a dog watches an ant.

When I pass close to him, carrying a heavy leather bucket of water to sluice the kitchen floor, he says: 'Stop right there, boy.'

I freeze.

'Look at me.'

Very deliberately I stare past him.

He says: 'Three questions. You call the innkeeper and his wife mother and father, but you look different. What's your story?'

'They found me in the river,' I say with a shrug.

'How?'

'My father used to be a fisherman, too poor for a boat, so he had to throw his nets from the shore. One day he was out fishing late and heard a noise in the bulrushes. He thought it was a kid or maybe a lamb and waded in to get it. It was me. I'd been wrapped in a cloth, put in a little reed boat and sent off down the river. Anyway, he brought me home to my mother and she . . . Well, I don't know. Maybe they liked me until Imi came along. Maybe she always thought I was a waste of space.'

'And now he's an innkeeper. Interesting. Second question: why are you so eager to please him and the woman? All they do is abuse you.'

'You made them look stupid last night so they'll take it out on me today,' I say. 'I just try to give them fewer excuses.'

'No one likes a cringer,' he says.

That hurts like a slap in the face. I don't say anything, but I feel a hatred for him so deep and strong that I can hardly breathe.

He nods. 'All right,' he says in that quiet voice. 'There's a bit of life in you, boy. Third question: what's changed?'

'What does the master mean?' I say, adjusting my tone. Submissive, sullen, sarcastic. I know how to annoy guests.

'The master means what he says,' he answers right back.

'Because the master stood up for me last night, I now have money,' I say. 'That's changed.' I take the tips from my purse and offer them to him. 'Does the master want a cut?'

'No.'

'Then I don't know what the master means.'

'The master will tell you, boy. When I arrived at the inn, you were curious about me. But from the moment you walked in last night, you've been keeping something from me. So what's changed?'

I try to hide my shock and start to bluster. 'I don't understand the master. I'm only a poor serving boy. The master knows how grateful I was. Am! I'm still grateful. That is what the master sees.'

My dumb act only amuses him. 'Anyone who can make this –' he holds up the little mud sphinx '– has got more than nothing going on between his ears. It's not grateful I'm seeing. It's something else. You went away to pick up your sister. You came back filthy and knowing. Now, how

30

do two little brats get dirty like that? From playing? I don't think so. From running? Maybe. From hiding?'

The shock must show again because he says: 'I can see through you like water, boy. Where were you hiding?'

'The City of the Dead,' I say, resistance crumbling.

His eyes narrow. 'Why would a cringer take his sister into the City of the Dead?'

I shake my head. 'She ran into it on the way back.'

'Why did she do that?'

'She said it was a short cut. And she thought it was funny that I was scared and she wasn't.'

He closes his eyes slowly. It's like his mind is chewing what I say to get the full flavour of it. Then the eyes open. 'But last night the little girl said she *had* been scared. Not of the dead or she would have stayed away. Why is that?'

I feel I've just walked into a trap that I knew was there all along. My mouth opens and closes.

'You tell me if you know so much,' I just about dare to say.

He shakes his head, then stands, those awful, thick arms heavy by his side.

'We'll get to the bottom of it, boy. I'm going for a little stroll, but we'll talk again when I come back.' And he walks out of the courtyard.

I'm so scared that I want to be sick.

9. In which I have a revelation

I try to settle down at the wheel to make more plates and beakers, but it's like he's put a spell on me. My hand can't shape the mud, can't make it rise and hollow into a beaker or thin into a plate.

This has never happened to me before, but my hands find something else to do. They pick up a lump of mud and start to shape it. A big, round head, piggy little eyes, nose like a broken rudder and an oddly full mouth. The Quiet Gentleman is the colour of mud anyway and no one seeing my model of him could mistake it for anyone else. Or mistake what I think of him.

I leave it on his bench, then retreat into my corner to think.

No one likes a cringer, the Quiet Gentleman says. Well, I'll show him what a cringer can do. From the way the tomb robbers were talking, it's clear he's brought something valuable with him, so when I go off to sweep his room, I check for soft earth where he might have dug a hole in the floor.

Nothing.

I run my hands over the walls, looking for missing bricks. All present and correct. A sudden burst of certainty sends me up a ladder to check the roof, but there's nothing up there either. Now I have to hurry, because how long can he be out strolling for?

Come on, come on . . .

My father comes out of the kitchen and scratches himself in the morning sunshine. He looks at me warily. I will him to notice that the courtyard has been cleaned from the night before and I've been out to get milk and bread.

He notices all right. He clears his throat, spits and says: 'Have you cleaned the shrine? It must be filthy. Take a broom down there and make sure you do a good job.'

It's like a sudden handclap of understanding. That's the place I should be searching.

Once, a long time ago, there must have been a temple or palace where our inn is now. If you dig in the courtyard you can find huge blocks of smooth stone just a little way down. All gone now but for a sort of hut with the goddess in it and that's our shrine.

I've never liked visiting the shrine. Now the gods are hiding, the statue down there is not much more than a stone corpse.

The light comes through the holes in the roof so she's always half lit, a worn lump of rock with an animal head and a woman's body. I think she was meant to be Sekmet, goddess of war and plague, but my father thought there were more commercial possibilities if she was one of the fertility goddesses, so he borrowed a chisel and hacked away until she looked a bit more like a hippo and said she was Tawaret, the goddess of making babies.

It worked, I guess, because Imi arrived, but I still think the goddess looks more like Sekmet, and a pretty angry Sekmet at that.

I stand in front of her. She doesn't look at me, just keeps on staring at the entrance with her badly painted eyes, like she's wondering where the crowds have gone. I put a coin between her stone feet and say: 'I'm going to look behind you. I hope it's not rude. Please don't give me the plague if you're Sekmet, or a baby if you're Tawaret. I don't know why the king killed you off, but it doesn't matter really, does it? You're still here and you're not going anywhere. Thanks.'

With a last glance up to see if she's angry, I squeeze into the space behind her. It's darker round here. No sand. A flagstone rocks slightly under my feet. I manage to lever it up and peer into the dark hole. I should have brought a taper from the kitchen fire . . .

The darkness moves. I know I'm not imagining it. There's just enough light to see something dark in there, as dark as water, gleaming like water, pouring itself like water, but with more purpose. And rustling with a dry sort of hiss.

Snake!

I jump back and the flagstone falls, but instead of a dull *whump* there's a wet crunch, then . . . nothing. I wait, motionless. Still nothing.

Swallowing my fear, I reach down and touch the dead snake's head, half severed by the edge of the falling flagstone, which I lift again and push back.

The first thing I find is a leather roll, wrapped tightly. The second is a small bag that is very, very heavy.

BOM-BOM-BOM-BOM-BOM. That's my heart.

My hands are trembling as I pick up the objects, then I squeeze out from behind the goddess into the half-light at the front of the shrine. And there is the Quiet Gentleman.

10. In which I accept that I have ruined my life forever

'So, boy,' he says, 'you found a way round my guard. Don't drop what you're carrying.' His voice is calm and level.

I was about to, I admit, just to show that I don't really care if I keep them or not. I can hardly breathe.

'Talk, boy.'

'Can't.'

'You just did.'

'Found these. Cleaning. They yours?' My voice is shaking and high. I hold out the leather roll and the heavy little bag. He takes the roll, which clinks like there's metal in it.

'You hang on to that,' he says, nodding at the bag.

'Why?'

'Just while we have a little chat. Now's the time to tell me everything you know.'

His voice is as flat as a knife. In that little shrine, with the sun slanting down through the holes in the roof, making everything striped, the truth comes pouring out of my mouth like grain from a slashed sack and it doesn't stop until there's no more truth to tell. The City of the Dead, the hiding, the rats, the men and all they said . . .

I finish and wait for the punishment I'm sure is coming, but the Quiet Gentleman just asks questions.

'So you think I'm a tomb robber, do you, mud boy?'

'I don't want to think anything,' I say.

'Why's that?'

'If you're a . . . you know what, you'll kill me.'

'So you know other tomb robbers?'

'No!' I almost shout.

'Then don't you worry about dying quite yet,' the Quiet Gentleman says pleasantly. 'I need you alive to answer a few more questions. These people you overheard: you never saw their faces?'

'Sort of. I think one of them was here the night you turned up. He left as soon as you arrived, but I recognised his voice.' I describe him, but can't see any change in the Quiet Gentleman's expression.

'Will you know the voices if you hear them again?'

I nod. 'And one was called Jatty.'

A pause. 'Did the other have a voice like a smear of cold vomit?'

I nod enthusiastically, but suddenly he's towering over me like a mountain. 'And why did you look for my things? To steal? To sell them to these men if they found me? Are you lying? Did they catch you? Did you do a deal with them to save your life?'

'NO! I just . . .' I gabble. 'I was scared to tell you in case you killed me. And then I was angry because you called me a cringer. I just – just wanted to look at what you had.'

He inhales like he's about to say something, then breathes out through his nose. When he finally speaks, I know it's not what he was going to say at first.

'Well, in that case, you'd better look before you die,' the Quiet Gentleman says. His eyes are like little dark slits, pushed up by his cheeks.

I open the bag. The object is wrapped in swathes of fabric.

'Careful, boy.'

And I unwrap a statue. It's the size of a kitten and the weight of a baby: a naked woman with the head of a cow and a sun balanced between her spreading horns.

'There,' the Quiet Gentleman says. 'Know what you're holding?'

'A goddess,' I whisper. 'One of the dead goddesses. Hathor.'

The gold is warm and buttery under my fingers and somehow it feels like there's give in it. I want to stroke it all over.

'Melt her down and you could buy this whole town. Think you should do that?'

I nod. Shake.

'It's too beautiful,' I say. 'It's worth more like this.'

'You're a strange one,' the Quiet Gentleman says. 'I should kill you, but you're more use to me alive than dead so here's how you pay me for your life. I want you to keep watching and listening. You see a group, any group, of three men in the street, you tell me.'

I nod.

'Know what will happen if you sell me short?'

I nod.

'Good, because now I won't have to watch the street, boy. I'll just have to watch you,' he says.

11. In which my father lets me down. Again. And uppances come

Next day, Imi's playing with her toys in the corner of the courtyard. She knows something's wrong with me because her eyes keep flicking from me to the Quiet Gentleman and back again.

My father sticks his head out of the kitchen and calls me over.

'How's it going with our friend over there?' he half talks, half mouths. He smells of onions and woodsmoke from cooking.

I shrug. 'He's fine.'

'Would you say he's taken a liking to you? Because your mother and I were wondering . . .'

'What?'

'Sometimes a gentleman likes the look of a boy and takes him on.'

'Takes him on?'

'As a companion. A servant. Remember, jobs are hard to come by in this day and age.'

'But I've got a job,' I protest. 'I work here.'

'There may be money in it,' he says.

I have never been more hurt or angry in my life.

'If you're so keen to get rid of me, why not just ask him? Better still, why not make a FOR SALE sign and hang it round my neck?'

My father smiles weakly. 'Come on, you know how things stand.'

'He doesn't want to take me on,' I say bitterly. 'He stares at me because he hates me.'

'What have you done?' he asks. Worried suddenly.

'I behaved like you.'

It's not a clever thing to say. My father's face twists and

he lifts his hand to hit me, then remembers the Quiet Gentleman and steps away.

'We need more wine,' he barks. 'Go and get it.'

He says it loud enough for the Quiet Gentleman to hear, who meets my eye and moves his head ever so slightly to the courtyard gate, giving me permission to go.

I can't quite read his face but there's something showing on it. Something like pity. Something like disgust at his ending up in a place like this.

The wine merchant lives on the other side of town in a shop that smells of vinegar and mould. There are small jars of the good stuff on shelves and huge jars of the crap stuff out the back, which is what we sell to our customers.

The only way I can carry one of these giant jars is on my head and it feels like it's trying to drive me straight down into the earth. The wine merchant loads me up and I stagger off like a two-legged camel, top-heavy and twice my normal height, down the dusty streets to the market square. I'm spotted by a gang of boys about my age who chuck pebbles at me, but just as I'm wobbling away from them, I hear another voice over their jeers and taunts.

'Sure this is the street?' it's saying and I'm sure it's the cold and sneery voice I heard in the City of the Dead.

'Course. I've been here before. The inn's just fifty paces the other side of the square. We're almost there. This way. No, that way.'

If I was in any doubt before, I'm certain now. That was the stupid one.

'That's no guarantee our friend is still there.'

They're right behind me. I can't drop the wine jar and run, so I walk as fast as I can in a sort of smooth waddle. The gang starts to jeer again, but at least I'm getting away. Then the wine inside the jar starts slopping from side to side and I have to swerve all over the place to keep it balanced. People are pointing and laughing, but I'm round the last corner now and can see the entrance to the inn and I'm pretty certain that I've managed to pull away from the three men.

I walk through the entrance into the little courtyard, looking for the Quiet Gentleman. He's there in his normal place, but for once he's not looking at me. He's listening to Imi who's somehow roped him into one of her crazy games.

'There you are!' I say, trying to sound normal, but feeling like I have to scream. 'Our friends have arrived!'

The Quiet Gentleman doesn't look up.

'HELLO, IT'S ME AND WE'VE GOT VISITORS!'

He looks up, head rolling on his neck like a boulder. He takes me in and then his eyes slip past me.

'Three visitors,' I say, but it's too late for the warning to be any good. The three men rush past me. I shout: 'IMI! WATCH OUT!' and then it all kicks off.

The Quiet Gentleman pushes Imi out of the way; the

huge pitcher of wine topples from my head, hits the ground and explodes. There's a chaotic muddle of bodies and shouts, until suddenly it all stops and one of the three men is lying on the ground with blood pouring from his nose, the Quiet Gentleman is holding a knife to the second man's throat – but the third has Imi by the hair and has his knife at her neck.

And then my parents come out of the kitchen to see what all the fuss is about. My mother opens her mouth to scream, but the man holding Imi snaps: 'Quiet or I kill the brat.'

My father claps a hand over my mother's mouth and holds her tight.

I'm paralysed with fear. I'm surrounded by shocked silence, apart from the moans of the man on the ground and the little bleats that come from my mother every time she breathes.

'Hello, Nebet,' the Quiet Gentleman says calmly. 'I see you've messed up again.' His eyes are just two dark slits and his lips are pulled back in a sort of snarl.

'I wouldn't say anything's exactly messed up,' Nebet says. I'm seeing the man with the cold and sneery voice for the first time. He's young and would be good-looking, but his little dark eyes are too close together and there's a twist to his mouth. 'Boy,' he says to me, 'close the courtyard gates and if you call out I cut off the pretty girl's nose. All right?'

I look at the Quiet Gentleman who gives a little nod.

When the gates are shut, the Quiet Gentleman gives a sorrowful shake of the head and says, 'Nebet, are you absolutely sure this is what you want?'

'Near enough, and just as soon as Bek manages to get off his knees we'll pick up what we came for and be on our way,' Nebet says.

'And what about Brother Jatty?' the Quiet Gentleman says. 'Want to see the colour of his blood?' Jatty must be the name of the man he's holding, the one with the worried voice. The Quiet Gentleman's knife is laid across the bump in his throat. Each time he swallows, the knife moves.

'Not really, but I don't care much,' Nebet sneers. 'Want to see the inside of this pretty little girl's throat?'

A little bead of blood appears at the point of the knife. My mother screams, properly this time, and tries to writhe out of my father's grip.

'Hurt the girl and I hurt Jatty. Then it'll be just you and me, Nebet,' the Quiet Gentleman says, 'and we all know how that will end: me staring down at you, and you staring down at your guts.'

'Shall we see?' Nebet says.

My mother's wailing now, sounding more like an animal than a human. And then I'm running. It's partly because I can't stand it and partly because I just know something's got to happen and I reckon no one can stop me.

I'm in the shrine and behind the statue and hauling up

the flagstone before I've taken a breath, and then it's back up into the sunshine and into the middle of the stand-off.

I rip open the bag and hold up Hathor so she gleams in the sunlight. No voice in my head, just a storm of madness.

'PUT YOUR KNIVES DOWN!' I scream so high my voice cracks. My breath is heaving like I've run round the town twice, but I feel as light as a feather. 'Put your knives down or this is going over the wall. I mean it!'

I look from Nebet to the Quiet Gentleman and I can see doubt in their eyes.

'Do that and you'll regret it,' the Quiet Gentleman says.

'I don't care,' I say. 'I'm warning both of you.'

A long pause. Horribly long. At last the Quiet Gentleman says, 'Nebet, the boy's shown us a way out. Shall we?'

They watch each other like dogs, then Nebet takes the knife from Imi's neck and the Quiet Gentleman takes his from Jatty's. They rest the blades in their open palms then lay them on the ground, all done slowly like a dance.

Jatty collapses. Imi runs across to her mother. I put the statue down and swallow.

'So now we talk,' the Quiet Gentleman says.

12. In which my fate is decided

The knives might be on the ground, but the danger isn't over. They leave Imi, but tie the rest of us up with strips torn from my father's best tunic and bundle us into the kitchen. The fire is out and the evening's bean stew is going cold.

Bek is the slow and stupid one the Quiet Gentleman knocked out. He's standing in the doorway, staring at us. His nose is swelling and his eyes are blackening. He stinks like an old drunk because he rolled in the spilled wine.

My mother is still crying; my father has screwed his face up and is pleading for our lives in a continuous, whining moan. Imi is all snot and sniffs and I'm wishing they would all shut up so I can make out what the others are saying in the next-door room. I can hear the sound of voices rising and falling and it's clear they're arguing. I hear words that don't seem to go together: horizon, workshop, and a name: Thutmose.

I'm thinking bitterly that if I'd just dropped the wine in the street and run here as fast as I could, I might have stopped all this happening. Now Imi is looking at me and I wish there was something I could do. I screw my face into a sort of smile. She disentangles my mother's clutching fingers, wriggles over to me and curls up in my lap.

Then the voices next door stop and Jatty appears, pushing Bek out of the way.

'All of you come next door,' he says, his eyes darting around nervously. 'Bek, untie them then keep watch at the courtyard gate. For the rest of you, things are going to change, but if you're good you'll have everything back as it was. One day.'

My mother starts to wail again. 'What have we done? How have we offended you? Is it the boy? Take him away. He's yours. He's been no good from the day we found him. Snivelled as a baby and never done a decent day's work in his life. Take him!'

'Right,' says Jatty, like a man trying to sound in control. 'Time to get serious. We could kill you all, but then we'd have to get rid of your bodies and that's always harder than people imagine. So we're going to make a deal. You and you' – he points at my parents with the tip of his knife – 'will stay here. You'll run the inn and look after Bek and Nebet who will also stay to make sure you behave.'

He nods at the Quiet Gentleman and continues. 'Hannu and I are going on a trip and we're going to take the girl as hostage. The boy comes too because he's old enough to understand the situation and, according to Hannu, he's good at looking after his sister and we might be busy.'

My mother screams. My father says: 'Hush, hush. It'll be all right. They won't be going far. Tomorrow everything

46

will be back to normal.' He appeals to the Quiet Gentleman. 'You're not going far, are you, sir?'

'We're going upriver,' Jatty says. 'We'll be away for as long as we need to be. It may be a month. It may be a year. But if word reaches us that you've talked, we're going to take this little girl to the Great River and throw her to the crocodiles. Are you clear about that?'

My father's skin is suddenly ashen. 'A month? A year?' is all he says.

'As long as it takes,' insists Jatty. 'You behave, nothing will happen. Talk and she dies.'

My father opens his mouth then closes it. He looks like a fish gulping for air.

'But why?' I say. 'You've got what you came for.'

Nebet glares at me. 'Which is what?'

'The statue.'

'Oh, that,' Jatty says. 'You think that's all we're after? No, that's more of a . . .'

'Enough!' the Quiet Gentleman snaps. 'The less everyone knows, the better.'

'Indeed,' Nebet says. 'And let no one forget it.'

And that's that. My mother is crying and clasping Imi, who looks really scared. My father takes me to one side and says: 'Look after her, boy, or I'll follow you through the Two Kingdoms and into hell.'

For the first time in his life, he looks like he means it.

And I have no idea where we're going. All I know is

that it's got something to do with the horizon, a workshop and a man called Thutmose.

13. In which my horizons open

We're travelling up the Great River on a cargo boat.

The river is milky smooth and earthy brown. There are fields on either side and dusty date palms droop in the heat. The boat is long and wide, low in the water, weighed down with cargo. Small fishing boats hug the banks. I see a horse running across a field of grass so green it makes me want to laugh with joy because the horse is beautiful and the rider looks so free.

I'm standing right at the back of the boat, where the giant helmsman nestles the steering oar under one massive arm. I stand next to him, my own arm wrapped round the sternpost. When the helmsman moves the rudder, eddies bloom and the water chuckles. I feel happy.

If I walk from one end of the boat to the other, climbing over the bales of hay, sacks of grain, jars of oil and wine, stacks of wood, rolls of linen, that's thirty big paces. If I walk from side to side, right in the middle where the mast is, that's ten big paces. The sailors look at me, call me mad monkey and laugh, but not unkindly. Even though my world is ten paces wide and thirty paces long, I feel free.

Then Imi joins me. Her skin is dull as if the sun has dried it. My happiness turns to dust and falls away. She needs looking after and that's my job, but I don't know what to do. The helmsman glances down at her.

'Water,' he says in a deep voice. 'The little girl needs a drink.'

I dip a ladle in the pitcher of water he keeps by him and hold it to Imi's lips. At first she presses her lips together, but I remember how she used to do that when she was a baby. Always started off by saying no. I persist. She takes a sip, then another, then takes the ladle and tips it into her mouth and drinks deeply and the relief I feel is like a drink of cool water.

'Where are we?' she says.

'On the river. The Great River.'

'Where are we going?'

I look up at the helmsman, who pulls the corners of his mouth down and shrugs. 'People it call it the Horizon, little girl, but if you want to call it by its full name, you can try the City of the Sun's Horizon, Home of the Only Living God on Earth, Akenaten, Champion of the Sun Itself and his Wife, Nefertiti, the Beautiful One is Approaching. It is the new capital of the Land of the Two Kingdoms.' He points to the river ahead of us. 'See that boat? See how high she rides? She's delivered her cargo and now she's heading back downriver to pick up more.'

'Is the boat a lady?' Imi asks.

'If you treat her right. If you don't then she turns into a –'

'Boy!'

The Quiet Gentleman's picking his way down the boat towards us. He beckons to me.

'Careful,' he says, when we're out of earshot. 'You'll have to keep her from talking and remember the story. I'm your uncle. We're going to find work in Horizon City. The king has spies everywhere on the river, don't forget.'

'But Jatty's talking to everyone,' I protest. It's true, though no one really wants to talk to him.

'Jatty's a fool and may have to be dealt with. Now, get your sister something to eat.'

'But suppose she asks me when we're going home? What do I say?'

'The better she behaves, the sooner she'll be going home. Tell her that.'

But it's hard to keep an eye on Imi all the time. Every evening, when we drop anchor, the sailors gather round a small brazier and cook the fish they've caught. They save Imi the best bits, sing her songs and tie knots for her and, while I know I should keep her away in case she talks about the fight at the inn, I can't when she seems to be happy with them.

Once I saw her ask the captain, who sits on a sort of throne just behind the mast, when she was going home. He looked embarrassed and shot a glance at the Quiet Gentleman. It took a while for me to work out that he was

50

frightened and didn't know what to say. It was then, I think, that I understood the Quiet Gentleman's power, his ability to scare, applied to everyone and not just me. I found the thought strangely comforting.

It's getting towards the evening of the second day and we've dropped anchor. Towns, villages and even fields have slid away behind us, though the land on either side is lush with reeds and grass. There's a gentle bend in the river so we can't see the boats behind us or ahead.

Imi's asleep. I'm looking up at the stars in the clearest sky I have ever seen and wondering how the frogs can make quite so much noise when the Quiet Gentleman comes and sits beside me.

'We've got a problem,' is all he says.

'Not of my making,' I answer.

'Not directly maybe,' he says. 'Jatty's made a friend at last.'

I did notice that Jatty was hanging out with one particular sailor. 'That skinny one with the face like a dog?' I ask.

'That's the one. Notice anything odd about him?'

'He wags his tail if you chuck him a bone?'

The Quiet Gentleman ignores my quite good joke. 'He works less than the others, but the captain never shouts at him.'

'So what?'

'He's a spy. Everything passes up and down the river: ships, goods, people, news. If the king wants to find out what's going on in his kingdom, he just has to plant snitches on boats and in harbours.'

'You think Jatty . . .'

'Either Jatty can't see a spy in front of his nose or he's playing a dangerous game. Either way, his new friend has a supply of wine and Jatty's trying to drink it all. That makes me worried too.'

'And what do you want me to do about it?' I snap. 'I don't want anything to do with Jatty. I've got my own worries.'

Just then something bumps against the side of the boat. The crewmen murmur and enough crowd to the side to tip the deck. Hannu's hand folds itself around my arm.

'That noise was a crocodile. Sailors feed them. Why do you think they do that?'

'I don't know,' I say.

He narrows his eyes. 'Let's look at this another way. Why do you think crocodiles always wait where the reeds on the riverbank are trampled down?'

I shake my head.

'It's because they know that's where the cattle drink. And why do you think crocodiles wait by the east bank of the river at sunset and the west bank at sunrise?' Hannu asks.

I shake my head again.

'So they can get close to the cattle behind the glare of the sun. Why am I telling you this?'

'Because you like cows?' I say.

'A clever tongue will only get you so far in this world, boy. Work it out.'

'Crocodiles are dangerous,' I say. 'The crew think that if they give them offerings, they won't eat them.'

'Good.'

'But the crocodile doesn't know that,' I say. 'It's stupid.'

'Crocodiles just want to eat,' Hannu says. 'Fill their bellies and they'll be less likely to eat you.'

He's giving off something. You know the heat of stones after a long, hot day? They give off a memory of warmth. What's coming off him, what's coming off his stillness is a memory of violence.

'It's not just crocodiles, is it?' I say. 'It's people too. Sometimes you have to give people what they want to get them off your back.'

'You need me to survive, boy,' he says in a thick voice. 'So when I ask, you give.'

There's no wind the next day. The boat tugs sluggishly against its anchor like a lazy fish on a line. The heat builds. The sun's like a metal plate in the sky. Imi's sitting quietly in the shade, feeding the ship's goat. Jatty wakes. He must have fallen asleep on a pile of ropes and they've left dents across his cheek. He's hungover, cross and, from the way he stretches, aching. He stumbles up to the ship's cook and asks for some bread, complains that it's stale then leans over the side of the boat and spits into the river.

I keep watching. He drinks water, asks for beer, drinks that too and cheers up. He walks round the boat, talking to the crewmen. Some of them are making knots and he has a go but so badly that everyone laughs. He drinks more beer, rests on a bale of linen, then gets up and finds Dogface and they move to the back of the boat.

No wind so no helmsman, just a little hen coop so the captain can have eggs for breakfast. The ship's cat likes to sleep on top of it, gazing down at the birds with white-toothed love.

I remember what the Quiet Gentleman said about giving him something so I crawl behind the hen hut. It's a narrow space littered with old vegetable peelings and droppings. The hens make gentle henny noises, but I can hear Jatty and Dogface over them.

'I'm still not clear what you want,' Dogface says. 'What's in it for me?'

'I told you,' Jatty says. 'Hannu's after something.'

'But what is Hannu after?' Dogface sounds mean and disbelieving. If he said it was a nice day, you'd check to make sure the sun was shining.

'He's not heading to the Horizon out of idle curiosity. He's plotting.'

'And the kids?'

'Cover. The boy makes things. You needn't worry about them.'

'What things?'

'Little model animals out of mud.'

'Could be blasphemous. The morality police will be interested in that. Might be worth something.'

'Turn 'em in, sell 'em, send 'em south, stuff 'em in a sack and drop 'em in the river. I don't care,' Jatty says. 'I just want to get Hannu.'

'So what's in it for you?' Dogface asks.

'Me? I'm just doing my duty for king and country,' Jatty says. 'Hail the king and hail the sun.'

'You want him out of the way. All right. Here's what we'll do.'

There's a creak and the boat heels slightly. Their conversation is cut short by the thunder of bare feet on the deck that starts before the captain even has time to shout: 'Up sail!'

Jatty and Dogface move away and when the deck is clear, I crawl out of my space and find Hannu, the Quiet Gentleman. He listens very carefully.

'Very good. That makes my decision easier.'

'What decision?' I ask.

He shakes his head as if I'm an idiot for even asking.

Later that day, when the boat is under way and the land

– bare desert now – is slipping past us, he gives me a small wineskin.

'I don't want that,' I say. 'I hate drinking.'

It's true. When you've seen as many drunks as I have, you tend to steer well away.

'Good. It's not for you,' the Quiet Gentleman says. 'But you're going to pretend that it is and tonight you're going to make sure Jatty sees it. And when he takes it off you, which he will, you're to say that it's from my secret supply of wine and if I find out it's gone there'll be hell to pay.'

'What then?'

'Then he'll drink it and that's what we want,' the Quiet Gentleman says.

'But . . .' I begin.

'But nothing. Have you forgotten what you told me? Stuff 'em in a sack and drop 'em in the river. Do you think he's joking?'

'But why? Where is this place we're going? And why are we going there? I need to know. Otherwise . . . it all just feels pointless.'

The Quiet Gentleman takes a deep breath as if he's controlling himself. 'All right,' he says. 'If it will help you.'

I nod.

'There's nowhere else in the world like Horizon City and there won't be ever again. It's the king's brainchild and the people there are the thoughts that flit around it.'

'But why?'

'He wanted to break the priests. The old kings were gods, but only because the priests made them so. He changed all that. He said there's one god, the sun, and he's the only one that can talk to him. It's a new city for a new idea.'

'But why are you going?' I say. 'And why am I here? I thought I was just a hostage, but Jatty said you brought me along because I can make things.'

'It's better you don't know.'

'I need to know,' I say. I try to talk like the Quiet Gentleman, level and patient, as if I can't imagine not having the answer. I feel a little surge of excitement – and terror – as I meet his eye and hold his stare, trying to imitate it.

'Well, well,' he says. 'We're getting close to the city and it's even changing mud boy into something new.' He squats suddenly, until his face is close to mine. I can hear the breath in his nose. 'You making things might help us, but it's not the point,' he says. 'The point is that you and me, boy, are going to commit a new type of crime together. It's going to be heinous.'

He's smiling and for the first time since I met him, he actually looks happy.

'But what?' My voice has gone hoarse and my mouth is dry.

'We're going to the Horizon and, when we get there, we're going to steal the light from the sun.'

He smiles and walks off, leaving me shaking.

14. In which an old god feasts

The moon is down when the Quiet Gentleman wakes me. I feel alert, but not fully. The sky is very black and the stars are blurred behind a river mist. It's cold, but I don't feel it.

The Quiet Gentleman's plan worked perfectly. I let Jatty see the wineskin and, as soon as he did, he snatched it from me. I pretended to protest and he just smiled his weak man's smile. I meant to stay up and see what happened, but I couldn't. I was suddenly too tired to do anything but curl up next to Imi and sleep.

'We've been moving all night and we're close to Horizon City,' the Quiet Gentleman whispers. 'It's worked out perfectly. We've dropped anchor in just the right place.'

The boat is rocking gently, creaking on its ropes.

'Feel that? A little river joins the Great River here. Makes for turbulence. The little river runs past the city of Taaud. Know who their god was?'

I shake my head.

'Sobek the crocodile. The priests honoured him by building his children a sacred lagoon. Biggest crocodiles I've ever seen. Hundreds of them. Thousands of them. So many and so well fed you could walk across the lagoon on their backs. Can you guess what happened when the old gods were banned?'

I shake my head.

'The king's soldiers broke the dam between the lagoon and the river and let the crocodiles out. A lot of them died, but a lot of them didn't. This whole stretch of river is full of monsters. Very hungry monsters.'

'I don't want to know,' I say.

'You don't need to know. All you have to do is keep watch, boy, while I do the deed.'

'But . . .'

'Remember what he was going to do to you and your sister.'

Too many big thoughts to turn into words. They just rush around in a panic, going nowhere. I should do something. I can't do anything. But is not doing anything really all right?

Jatty's a huddled shape lying against the side of the boat, close to us all in the bows. He's snoring quietly.

The Quiet Gentleman takes something out of his pocket and there's the sound of string snapping. I tell myself that Jatty was going to kill us and this is our last chance to stop him and this is to protect Imi, it's all to protect Imi, and only a coward would do nothing when there was a chance to stop it.

It's only when the Quiet Gentleman slips the thin string around Jatty's neck that I look away and clamp my hands over my ears. Next thing I know, the Quiet Gentleman's leaning over the side of the boat, dropping Jatty's body into the water so gently he never makes a sound. Then he's just a shape, floating, bobbing and swirling away as the current takes him.

It's not long before I hear a splash and see the flash of white in the river as the first crocodile finds him.

Then another.

And another.

I turn and my heart nearly stops beating. Imi's standing there. She's looking at me with eyes so wide I can see the stars in them.

'He's gone,' she says.

'Yes,' I say. 'Jatty's gone.'

'Where?' she asks.

'I think the old gods have found him,' I say. 'It's all right. We're arriving at the City soon. It's going to be exciting, Imi. It's going to be a new start.'

I can see her mouth about to form another word, so I add: 'He was going to do bad things to us, Imi. Now he can't. Just remember that. Now we've got a chance of surviving.'

'Where?'

'In Horizon City.'

Why do those words fill me with such dread?

15. In which I smell a smell and see a sight

Sunrise brings more heat and more worries: worries that Dogface is going to corner Imi and get her to talk; worries that he'll corner me and get me to talk; worries that someone saw what happened to Jatty.

But no one cares. In fact, far from suspecting us, the sailors comfort us for the loss of our brother and say he did a lot of this (pretending to drink from an invisible wineskin). They hope he drowned before the old crocs got him because being eaten alive is a terrible way to go. The Quiet Gentleman spends the morning on his own and is treated with respect, as a man mourning his travelling companion should be. I want to ask him what he meant the other day when he said we were going to steal the light of the sun. At the time I thought he must be joking, but when did the Quiet Gentleman ever joke? His face is as dead as stone. I don't dare say a word to him.

Then, in the afternoon, after a day of moving forward steadily under sail, the wind drops again and I begin to smell a dreadful stink.

It's like the town dump at home, only thicker and stronger, and the Great River looks like it's been carpeted with rotting vegetables and other things that I don't even want to talk about mixed up in its filth. A dead cow goes bobbing past, and a calf, their legs pointing up at the sky like the legs of an upturned table. You would never think that there was that much stuff in the whole world to throw away and we're sailing through it.

I know what's coming when the Quiet Gentleman walks over to me and says: 'Get ready, boy. The city's just round the next bend. You'll see it first thing in the morning.'

And here's something else I know: I'm arriving at the rest of my life.

It's just after dawn when the crew breaks out the oars and we round the bend in the river. My first glimpse of the city is of smudged brightness, dim white shapes in the mist behind a forest of masts. A mass of houses, more than I have ever laid eyes on.

'It's incredible,' I say. 'I've never seen anything like it.'

The Quiet Gentleman snorts. 'That's just the northern suburbs, boy. There! Look upriver.'

And I see it. The sun breaks through the mist to reveal white walls, high towers, bright flags; a great palace that emerges and then disappears into the mist. On this side of it is a vast temple, bigger than my entire hometown. Behind the river palace there's another temple, and another palace, and clustered all round, a jumble of rooftops grovelling at the base of those glaring, bright, cliff-like walls.

'It's amazing, isn't it?' I say to Imi.

She squints. 'It's very bright,' she says.

'It's the house of the king and the home of the sun,' the Quiet Gentleman says. 'Now close your mouth and stop gawping. We're here for a while so you'd better get used to it.'

He points further upriver. Our boat is almost nudging other boats, all crammed with bellowing cattle, wailing sheep, baskets of geese, pyramids of stone. In one, a horse is tethered to a sort of platform, taut ropes holding it in place, then we're through and make our way slowly past the palace walls to the dockside, where a forest of cranes joins the forest of ships' masts and the quay is piled with goods.

On-board, the sailors are all getting ready to unload, all apart from Dogface. He's waiting for the gangplank to fall so he can be first ashore. I elbow the Quiet Gentleman and nod towards him. He nods back.

'Get your sister,' he says. 'Pick her up. Get ready to run. This is where Dogface will turn us in, if that's his plan. We have to make ourselves scarce.'

As soon as the boat bumps the quay, before it's secured by ropes, before the skinny porters who are massing on the quayside march on-board, the Quiet Gentleman has leapt over the side and is waiting with arms raised for Imi. I follow, my feet hitting the ground with a solid jar. After three days on the boat, it feels too hard.

'This way. Keep low!' The Quiet Gentleman points to a

row of waiting porters with dull eyes and scabbed backs. City slaves.

'Hey!'

The shout comes from the boat. The Quiet Gentleman glances over his shoulder then says: 'Run!'

I run with Imi in my arms. 'Look behind us. What's going on?' I pant.

'There's a man on the boat pointing at us and shouting,' she says, her voice broken by the jogging.

In spite of his size, the Quiet Gentleman moves like a dancer between piles of stone and jars of oil, then slips sideways. There's a gate into the city right in front of us, but he's leading us away from it towards one about a hundred paces further on. I see his reasoning – if Dogface gets anyone's attention, the guards at the nearest gate are within shouting distance and could stop us.

A huge tree trunk has just been lifted on to rollers and is blocking our way. There's a drummer standing nearby beating time. Some of the slaves are working the rollers with long levers, digging them in and pushing on the drumbeat. Others are harnessed to the trunk, their muscles standing out like twisted ropes, and the overseers are keeping everyone in line with whips. But the trunk is long and moving slowly; it's going to take ages to pass. We're stuck.

'What's happening?' I ask Imi again.

'The man on the boat's still looking, but I don't think he

can see us. No, wait! He's pointing. I can see soldiers. I can see their spears. They're coming this way!'

Suddenly one of the slaves slips and falls in front of a trundling roller. He shouts and tries to twist away, but too late! The roller catches his trailing leg. An awful splintering crunch is drowned out by his scream. The slave behind him stops pushing, then the one behind him, but they're still pushing on the other side. I can see the roller slew around; the trunk lurches, then stops dead.

'Come!'

The Quiet Gentleman clambers over the trunk; I slither underneath, pushing Imi in front of me, and then we're past and all running to the gate. People are surging in the other direction to see why the drums have stopped and we battle through them and out the other side. Then we're in sight of the gate, and then we're through.

We're in the City of the Sun's Horizon. We're in the city of the god.

16. In which the Quiet Gentleman changes names

If I thought Imi would be frightened, I was wrong. As we walk along the street, her sitting pretty on my shoulders, I can feel her excitement. People are staring – she's waving to them and it doesn't seem to bother her that no one waves back. The Quiet Gentleman won't have any of it.

'Put her down,' he says. 'We've just escaped the king's guard at the docks. Do you want to show them where we are?'

I'm embarrassed. I should have thought. Imi slides down off my shoulders and takes my hand.

We're heading away from the river and into a narrow street of small homes. At first you think the houses are arranged in lines, but after a while the streets start to wander in loose curves and the houses pile up on each other, as if the streets got lost or people just stopped caring. It reminds me of the City of the Dead, but instead of crumbling mud bricks, here all the houses are painted white. Every twenty paces or so, the sound of hammering comes from a house, or the *chuck, chuck, chuck* of woodworking tools. There are piles of sawdust in the street and smoke from smithies. But I notice one thing: no one here smiles or greets anyone else. They hurry past on their business with their eyes lowered, apart from the ones who look on suspiciously.

The Quiet Gentleman darts down a side street. I smell beer brewing, cooking smells – home, in fact – and there, on the corner, is an inn with tables, benches and a woven awning against the sun. A few people are seated there, some drinking with their breakfasts, others just passing the time.

'What are we doing?' I ask.

'We'll take a seat and we'll wait. This is where the workshops are. We're going to find a craftsman.'

'Thutmose?' I say.

'You were listening.'

'Is he a craftsman?'

'A very special one. But I don't want to ask people in the street about him because of all the spies,' the Quiet Gentleman says. 'Just remember this. I am not Hannu. I am not the Quiet Gentleman – yes, I know what you call me. From now on call me the man we killed. My name is Jatty.'

'But we can't! It means every time anyone says your name I'll think of him.'

'No. You will remember that if I hadn't killed him, you'd be arrested by now and about to face the king's police. Or dead. Got that?'

'I suppose so.'

'What's my name?'

I open my mouth, but nothing comes out. Then it's like a furnace opens behind the Quiet Gentleman's eyes and black heat scorches me. Imi grabs my hand and squeezes it tight.

'What's my name?' he says again.

'Jatty,' I say. But it costs me. I can still remember the gurgle in his throat when the rope went round it, the drumming of his heels on the deck, the wet opening of the water as he slid in, the splash and grunt as the crocodiles took his body in the black water.

'Good. Does she understand?'

I look at Imi and will her to nod. After a while she does, slowly.

The innkeeper bustles over to our table. 'Now, what can I do for you on such a fine morning? Bread and beer for the gentleman? And for the young people?'

His eyes dart from the Quiet Gentleman to me then to Imi and back again. He's trying to size us up in a way I know all too well from living at the inn.

'Bread and beer will do me well,' the Quiet Gentleman says. 'And milk for my nephew and niece.'

But the innkeeper lingers. 'Passing through?' he asks.

'Travelling south to see my sister, but I'm hoping to pick up some work along the way.' The Quiet Gentleman talks differently when he lies, I think. More musical. Less flat.

'Got a trade?'

'I've got skills,' the Quiet Gentleman says with a tilt of his head.

'Oh yes?' The innkeeper folds his arms. 'What skills?'

'Special ones.'

This is a grown-up way of talking: the words have another meaning underneath them.

'Well, you're in the right place, but I warn you, even the finest craftsmen are having trouble these days,' the innkeeper says. 'When the queen's palace was going up –

that was last year – the workshops were begging for craftsmen. Now the gossip is all about how she's refusing to move out of the king's palace at all, so all work's stopped and they're laying people off. Unless they've got something very special to offer.'

'Oh, I've got something very special,' the Quiet Gentleman says.

Then Imi pipes up, 'And so does my brother.'

'Shut up, Imi,' I say.

'But it's true,' she insists.

'No, it isn't.'

'He makes animals,' she says. 'And they talk to me.'

The silence gathers like the air before a clap of thunder, but the crash doesn't come. Instead, the innkeeper laughs. He pats Imi on the head and moves off towards the back of the inn to shout out our order.

'Sort her out,' the Quiet Gentleman says to me and he settles down on the bench, leaning against the wall behind him. Only his hands resting by his side move, like animals that twitch in their sleep.

17. In which I draw a blasphemous hippopotamus

I take Imi down to the other end of the table.

'You mustn't talk that way,' I say. 'This isn't like home.'

'I know it isn't,' she says. 'It isn't home because it's somewhere else.'

'No. I don't mean it's not like home because it isn't home. I mean . . . we have to be different here. We have to behave differently. It's like a game where we say as little as possible because we don't want people to recognise us. So every time you tell someone I can do something special, that's going to make them notice us and that's a bad thing. Did you understand that?' I ask.

Now she looks at my eyes, as if the answer is there.

'Yes?' she says cautiously.

I smile. 'That's right. It draws attention to us.'

'Because it will make people look at me?'

'That's right, Imi. Good.'

'I don't think I want people to look at me anyway. They're not very friendly here, are they?'

She makes a face. Food arrives. The innkeeper smiles at her and rubs a knuckle against her cheek.

'Pretty girl,' he says.

'My aunt says that, but I can't hear her,' Imi says.

'What? Why? Gone deaf?'

'No. She's a long way away.'

The innkeeper chuckles uncertainly and moves off, flicking at flies with a cloth.

'I think that was fine,' I say. 'And remember, the Quiet Gentleman's name is Jatty.'

'Like the man you dropped in the river.'

Relief to panic in a thumping heartbeat. 'Don't say that either,' I hiss between gritted teeth.

'All right,' she answers brightly. 'After breakfast, will you draw me an animal?'

I give up. After we have eaten, I find a stick and draw a hippopotamus standing by a palm tree and a crocodile who's come by to eat some dates. Then a camel turns up and, just as the camel and the crocodile are about to start a complicated fight, a dirty bare foot lands right in the middle of the drawings and scuffs them over.

I scramble to my feet and come face to face with a boy about my age standing with two hard-looking men with shaven heads. One has a scar down the left side of his face from his temple to his jaw. It draws the corners of his eye and mouth down so he looks as if he's sneering.

The boy stares down at his foot, as if he's surprised at what it's done.

'What did you do that for?' I bluster.

I feel the bulk of the Quiet Gentleman move close behind me. His hands land on my shoulders and start to squeeze.

'Let it go,' he says and looks at Scarface. 'Good morning. How does the day find you?'

'Good enough. That boy of yours wants to watch himself.'

'Can you tell me why?'

'All writing, all stories, all images are to be created only by licensed operators,' Scarface answers. 'No exceptions.'

'Is that a new rule?'

'The god makes new rules every day in the City of the Sun's Horizon. You'd be wise to make it your business to find out what they are. Some might say making an image of an animal is blasphemous and the punishment for blasphemy is death.'

'I'll make a note of that, brother,' the Quiet Gentleman says, suddenly all friendly. 'My thanks to you and your young friend for showing us the error of our ways. Now, won't you sit down and share a jug of beer with me?'

'That depends. We heard there was a man here with something to offer.'

'Could be,' the Quiet Gentleman answers. 'Something to offer to the right man.'

'We could sit and talk about it,' Scarface says, 'if you would give me your name.'

'Jatty,' the Quiet Gentleman says.

Imi nods wisely and repeats: 'Jatty.'

'And Jatty is from . . .?'

'Jatty is from where he was last. Downriver, as it happens.'

'We got word about a man called Jatty from downriver, although he was travelling with two other men, not two little kiddies.'

'Plans change,' the Quiet Gentleman says. 'There was another man with us, but he left the boat in the middle of the night. A waste of space called Hannu. A common thief. He won't be missed.'

Imi is holding my hand. I give it a warning squeeze. The Quiet Gentleman calls the innkeeper over and then he and Scarface sit side by side on the bench, backs to the wall, eyes to the alleyway. All the other guests at the inn have melted away.

'You're a man of influence, I see,' the Quiet Gentleman says.

'Even though my master's secrets aren't the kind that can be stolen, it's best to encourage people to keep their distance. He's the king's master craftsman. His ears have heard the king's wisdom and his eyes have drunk the queen's beauty. He is one of the few men who have been allowed near her in the palace, but let us just say that times are hard and he is looking for men with new . . . skills.'

'I have a craft of my own,' the Quiet Gentleman says. 'So I have no need to steal your master's. His secrets are safe with me, but do you think that mine will be safe with him?'

Scarface narrows his eyes. 'We were given to understand that our friend Jatty would be able to show us something that proved who he was, and another thing to prove he had skills. If you can show me these, then we all know where we stand.'

Without taking his eyes off Scarface, the Quiet

Gentleman reaches into his tunic and takes out a pouch that looks like the one Jatty kept tied round his waist. He produces a bit of broken pot. Scarface nods and his companion walks over with a small wooden box. Inside the box, wrapped in fabric is a similar-looking shard. The Quiet Gentleman holds his out and Scarface does the same and they press them together. The two pieces join perfectly.

'There now,' Scarface says. 'Always good to meet a fellow craftsman. The city has been crying out for one such as you for a long time. And now for the other? The proof of your skills?'

'That is for Thutmose and Thutmose alone. It is not a thing to be shown in a public place.'

Scarface looks at the Quiet Gentleman. 'I see. Very well. Follow me.'

18. In which I discover my future

Thutmose, the king's master craftsman, looks like a tiny bird. His head is set forward on his scrawny neck and his nose pecks the air when he talks. His small dark eyes are always darting from left to right.

Thutmose owns a whole street. At one end is his house, the rooms set around a courtyard, and his workshops fill the other buildings. There are the rooms where craftsmen carve wood, rooms where they carve stone, rooms full of paints, and then there's the room where they make heads.

Once Thutmose has checked out the fragment of pottery for himself, he leads us through the rooms, his head pecking the air to the right and left like a hen looking for insects.

'Yes, indeed, this is for the king's palace. This is for the queen's palace. This is for the princess's state rooms. This is for the . . . never mind about that. This is for the north palace. Those paints are for the sanctuary of the Lesser Sun Temple . . . What do you think? What do you think?'

His voice is fussy. His little black eyes are sharp.

'Most impressive,' the Quiet Gentleman says. 'And out of all these splendours, what is the great craftsman most pleased with?'

'Pleased? Pleased? You think I am pleased? You understand nothing about the craft,' the old man snaps. 'This is my greatest work, yes indeed. But do you think I am pleased with it now, or ever will be?'

On a bench there is a tall object draped with a cloth. Thutmose whips the cloth off to reveal a life-size head, roughly carved in pale stone. The high crown with the cobra rearing above it means it's royal, and I think it's a woman, even though the features are unfinished and blurred. The head leans forward on a long, delicate neck so it seems to be straining for something.

'So,' the Quiet Gentleman says, 'is that it? Is this

75

Thutmose's famous unfinished business?'

'What do you know about it?' the old man snaps.

'Only what I have heard. People say that Thutmose, the greatest craftsman in the world, was commissioned to make the head of the queen, but her beauty defeated him.'

'It's not her beauty that defeated him. It's these new materials we have to work with. This soapstone. This gypsum. This rubbish. They won't let us use stone – the king has decreed that is the old way. Everything must be done in the new way. The truth is simpler: he built his city in a place with no good stone and can't afford to ship it in by river.'

He stands in front of the head and runs his fingers over the hollow of the cheek, the dip of the eye socket. My fingers move as if they have a life of their own, imitating his.

'What do you think?' he says to the Quiet Gentleman, but I answer. I can't stop myself.

'It's the most beautiful thing in the world,' I say.

Silence. The master craftsman snaps his head round and tilts it to one side. His glittering little eyes take me in. Dust swirls in the sunlight.

'The boy's in love,' one of the craftsmen sniggers.

'Whose boy?' Thutmose asks.

'He's with me,' the Quiet Gentleman says.

'What is he? Your child? Your slave? Your companion?'

'None of those things, Thutmose. He is my gift to you.'

'What?' I can't stop myself blurting it out. 'But you . . .'

'Silence!' the Quiet Gentleman snaps.

He's standing close to Imi and places one enormous hand on each of her shoulders. I read it as a threat and close my mouth.

Thutmose stalks across the floor towards me.

'When people want to buy my attention, it's the custom to bring something a bit more conventional than a boy,' he says. 'But perhaps Jatty is not a conventional man.'

'I have an ordinary gift, if you would prefer it,' the Quiet Gentleman says. 'Here.'

He reaches into his leather shoulder bag and brings out the golden statue, as heavy as a baby and worth more than my hometown. Thutmose's eyes glitter.

'The goddess Hathor,' he says. 'Old. Too dangerous to keep like this. Have to melt it down. Even so, the boy would have to be a very special brat to compete with that. What does he do? Bleed rubies? Cry diamonds? Piss gold?'

'May we talk alone?' the Quiet Gentleman asks.

With a quick peck of the head, Thutmose leads us down a corridor and into an empty courtyard. He sits on the edge of a sun-bleached wooden bed frame in the shade, and gestures to the Quiet Gentleman to sit on another. A slave appears with a large fan which he starts to wave.

Imi and I stand as close as we can to it. It's hotter here than at home. The sun is beating down into the courtyard and the sky is a polished copper dome.

'Talk,' Thutmose says.

'We have heard that times are difficult in the City of the Sun's Horizon,' the Quiet Gentleman says calmly. 'We have heard that the king and the queen are at war; that the king may ride like the sun from one end of the city to another every day, but nothing gets done; that building work has ground to a halt so there are no more commissions for the king's own master craftsman; that the way back into royal favour is through the queen and not the king . . . And that this child may be able to show you that way. That is why I believe this gift is worth even more than gold or rubies.'

'You heard that in the north?' Thutmose asks. His whole manner of speaking has changed. Not as fussy; more direct.

'And before I was in the north I was somewhere else, and somewhere else before that. News travels,' the Quiet Gentleman says.

'But what about this gift? First of all, does it have a name?'

'Not as far as I know,' the Quiet Gentleman says. 'He's a foundling. I call him mud boy.'

'And his value?'

'He makes things from mud that look as if they're alive. I have heard that is also the new way in Horizon City.'

Thutmose smiles thinly, then shakes his head. 'This brat makes things? I have workshops full of people who can make things.'

'He's different. I believe the old gods talk to him, but in a way that could be put to use.'

'Now I've heard it all! Enough! I can't be bothered with any of this. We need to talk business and, while we sort that out, the boy and girl can work.' His eyes slide over to Imi, who smiles. 'The girl goes to the kitchen and the boy works in the yards. You,' he says to me. 'Find Sethi, the little runt who brought you in, and tell him that Thutmose wants to see what you can do with gypsum in the yard. Are you clear?'

Imi is swept off and I look dumbly at the Quiet Gentleman, suddenly desperate to cling on to anything familiar, even if it is the man who has just given me away. He doesn't look at me.

I walk back through the workshops, dragging my feet, not really looking around me and barely taking in my surroundings. That's it? The plan was that I was meant to make things for Thutmose, but he's not interested? Where does that leave me now?

Sethi is waiting for me. He stares at me and I stare back, unable to think of a thing to say.

'Have you come to take my job?' he says in a hopeless voice. I see him properly for the first time: his skin is dull and wrinkled and his eyes are bloodshot.

I shake my head. 'I think it's a sort of test.'

'That's what they said to me,' Sethi says dully. 'What's your name?'

'Most people call me boy.'

His face lights up. 'But that's what they call me too,' he says. 'We're like each other.'

I follow him out of a side door and into a small, stifling courtyard – four walls of mud bricks that trap the sun's heat like an oven. In the middle of the courtyard is a rough pile of yellowish rocks, half my height. To the right of the pile is a large granite bowl with a sort of blunt-ended club lying by it.

'You know what to do?' Sethi says in his lifeless voice. 'You have to break the rocks, like this.'

He drops a lump of the yellowish stone into the bowl where he pounds it with the club. It crumbles quite easily.

'It's got to be as fine as flour,' Sethi says. 'And we've to get through that pile by sunset or we work all night too.'

One of us pounds away at the stone while the other scoops it up and puts it into sacks, and then we swap jobs. I don't know which is more terrible: the blistering pain of smashing the rocks, or the clouds of dust that rise up when you pour it into the sacks.

We go at it until it gets dark. The dust stings my eyes and clogs my nose and mouth. I get blisters on my hands, which hurt, and then they burst and it's even worse. Then the dust gets into them and that's worst of all.

When we've finished, Sethi drags me to a water tank in the corner and we use the scoop to wash each other down. He shows me a straw mattress under a workbench and says he will let me share it with him. There's no sign of the Quiet Gentleman, there's no sign of Thutmose and there's no sign of Imi. There's just me, Sethi and a flat loaf of bread and a bowl of lentil mush. A guard locks the door and the shutters on the windows so we eat in the stifling darkness.

Sethi falls asleep, but misery keeps me awake. I now see that the time on the boat was like a held breath and this, now, is my new life. Thutmose isn't interested in me. I'm just a prisoner, a hostage whose only purpose is to stop my parents from talking.

19. In which I learn a thing or two

The next morning we're sent to the furnaces on the outskirts of town.

Sethi says the rocks we crushed make the gypsum, which is what they use here instead of stone. Gypsum is a sort of plaster – soft as mud when it's wet but you can carve it like stone when it's dry. It sounds odd to me – stone should be stone and mud should be mud – but I'm too tired and sore to give it much thought. It's just a relief to be walking.

We head for the columns of smoke that rise above the rooftops to the east. All the houses look the same with their white walls and gaping square windows. The streets are almost empty and the few people I see keep their heads down as they scurry past. We walk past a slaughterhouse that stinks and a tannery next door that stinks worse and then we come to the furnaces.

They stand alone in a dusty courtyard: four beehive ovens surrounded by piles of wood and white stone. There's a bitter smell in the air. A boy of about my age is standing by the door of the first oven and a man is asleep in the shade on a low bedstead. The boy looks as if he's been shrivelled by his work: his skin is dark, patched with lighter burns, and there's nothing to the rest of him.

'When's the next batch ready?' Sethi calls out.

The boy looks at us over his shoulder and shrugs.

'Does the boss know?' Sethi jerks his head towards the sleeping man.

'Maybe, but leave him be. He was drinking last night. Who's this?' He nods at me.

'People call me boy,' I say.

Just like Sethi, he says: 'They call me that too. We must be brothers.'

'His real name's Lolkerra,' Sethi says. 'It means Owner of Many Sheep.'

Lolkerra puffs out his skinny chest and nods.

'So where are your sheep now?' I ask. It's nasty, but something in his desperation and pride touches a raw place deep inside me and makes me want to hurt him.

His shoulders drop. 'Gone,' he says. 'Taken by your soldiers when they killed my family.' I notice he says *your soldiers* and I want to say *not mine*, but I've created the distance between us.

The man wakes up and yells at us to be quiet, then at Lolkerra to fetch him some water.

'And who are you?' the man asks as his eyes unsquint and fall on me.

'I'm with him,' I nod at Sethi.

'Where are you from?'

'The north.' And then, because I think some kind of explanation is needed, I add: 'I came with Jatty.'

'Jatty from the northern brotherhood?' he says. 'Well, well. He's been trying to get in with Thutmose these past three years. Tell him to be careful and tell him to look out for me. He owes me from a job we did up there.'

I feel the sweat on me freeze. 'Oh, I don't know if it's that Jatty,' I say.

'Course it is. Only one Jatty. Now, what did you want? When's the next load due? It'll be ready tomorrow.' He seems to be in better spirits now that I'm feeling overwhelmed by panic. 'Jatty, eh? Can't wait to see him again.'

20. In which I miss the Quiet Gentleman

As soon as I can, I get Sethi to lead me back to the workshops. If the man at the furnaces knows Jatty, he'll know the Quiet Gentleman isn't Jatty. I've got to warn him.

It's not as easy as I think. When I try to get into the workshops, the man guarding the door won't let me in, and when I say I want to talk to Jatty, he tells me that Jatty's left. Then he cuffs me across the head and tells me not to ask questions unless I want to end up floating face down in the Great River.

Scarface comes to the door to find out what all the fuss is about, and when I tell him, he says with a smirk that Thutmose has sent Jatty off to look for quarries in the mountains.

'Quarries?' It's the first I've heard of it.

'What's it to you?' He steps forward menacingly.

'Nothing,' I say hastily. 'He'll be back though? He's not gone away for good?'

'He'll be back if he knows what's good for him,' Scarface answers.

And I've no time to think about this properly because we now have to mix a load of plaster. Sethi shows me how to scoop the powder into a large stone trough. Then, when it's about half full, I carry half a dozen buckets of water over from the tank in the corner of the courtyard and empty them into the trough. Then he hands me a sort of cross between a paddle and a spade and tells me to get mixing.

It's all right to begin with. The paddle moves easily at first, but as the mixture gets stiffer and stiffer, my arms start to ache and then my back. Soon my shins are bleeding from knocking into the side of the trough and sweat drips from my forehead into the plaster.

'Now you have to put it in the buckets.' Sethi points to them. 'Fill them then take two to the workshops – one in each hand. Go on!'

The rest of the day passes in a haze of pain and exhaustion. If I thought I was sore yesterday, it's nothing to how I feel today.

At one point I look up and see Thutmose standing in the doorway, watching me.

He hands me a bowl. 'I want a thicker batch,' he says.

I put some powder in the bowl, then add water a drop at a time and work the mixture into a paste. Thutmose turns the bowl upside down. The plaster slithers out.

'How can I work with that, boy?'

'You want to work it with your hands?'

'Indeed, what else?'

I mix another batch, but this lot stiffens too quickly. It's interesting though, because there was a moment when the

85

white paste became almost the same consistency as my mud, but smoother and somehow stronger.

Same amount of powder, a splash more water. It feels good. I take a lump of it out of the bowl and knead it with my fingers.

The wheel turns, the wheel burns . . .

I feel a shape emerging under my fingers.

I crush it. What use is that going to be? I crush the shape and I crush my hopes. I take the bowl to Thutmose and hand it to him without looking, then I get back to work.

Two more loads. The sun goes down. I wash and stagger back to the stuffy workshop, but I'm too tired to eat my bread and lentils. Sethi is already asleep on the mattress and very soon I am too.

21. In which I lose an ache and gain a worry

The next day is worse than the one before, but when I wake up on the third morning, I'm aching in a different way. My body is hardening. I'm hardening.

That evening, after work, I get permission to visit the kitchens where Imi is working. The cook's assistant, who is about the same size as the cook's left leg, tries to throw me out until she discovers I'm Imi's brother. Then her face softens and she lets me into the small kitchen smelling of smoke and spice and hot oil.

'She's such a treasure. Look at her sitting there, doing her best to help, the precious little thing. Such a shame she'll be sent off to learn her trade as a musician or a dancing girl, but then . . .'

'Quiet, fool.' The cook's voice is thick and smooth like oil. She is sitting on the floor, plucking a goose. Imi is sitting by her, shelling peas.

With a glance at the cook to make sure it's all right, Imi holds me like she'll fall down if she lets go. Her face has lost its pinched look from not eating or drinking, but there is something dead in her expression that perhaps only I can see.

'How are you?' I ask.

'It's nice here,' Imi says. 'Everyone's very kind. I'm so lucky.'

This is like someone imitating Imi, not Imi herself.

'And they're going to teach you music?'

'Yes. If I'm good I can play for rich men when I'm older,' she says.

'Oh. We'll be away by then,' I say, my voice shaking. 'I'm sure of it and then we'll be home and back with Mother and Father.'

The cook's assistant makes a *tsk-tsk* noise. 'Why of course,' she says. 'You won't have to worry about learning how to play any silly old harp then. But just in case . . .'

The cook interrupts. 'Just in case, we'll make sure you

can pluck with the best of them,' she says. She pulls a great handful of downy feathers from the goose's breast and throws them up. They float, they sink, they catch the heat from the oven and are tossed up again to the kitchen's rafters before drifting down once more.

'Catch them, little girl, catch them.' The words ooze from her mouth and with joyless skips, Imi tries to catch feathers that dance away from her little hand.

She's changing before my eyes and I can't stand it. Seeing her has made me realise that this is no place for her or me. I'll wear myself out crushing gypsum and she'll go mad in the kitchens. I've got to get her out of here. But how?

22. In which the Quiet Gentlemen returns

Excitement! Panic! Disaster! Hope! The Quiet Gentleman is back from the mountains, but he doesn't look too happy and he doesn't look too well.

It's night and I'm deeply asleep when Scarface kicks me awake. I unglue my eyes to see the Quiet Gentleman and three other men standing in the flickering candlelight. Two look grey and pinched with exhaustion and the third has his arm in a dirty sling. One entire side of his tunic is bloodied from shoulder to waist.

'Get them water!' Scarface orders. 'Then go to Thutmose's private quarters and tell him they're back. Just him. Be quick and be quiet.'

I shoot a desperate look at the Quiet Gentleman and hope he'll call me over – I need to tell him that someone knows the real Jatty – but he waves me away. I run through the empty workshops and down the corridor to Thutmose's quarters, shout at a servant that he's wanted and run back, desperate to get to the Quiet Gentleman, but it's no good. He's tending to the wounded man, and then Thutmose appears and my chance has gone.

Now, I know there's a time for talking and a time for listening, and this is a time for listening. I fetch water for washing and beer for drinking and hope people forget I'm even there.

'So,' Thutmose says, 'don't tell me that you've failed to honour your promise. Tell me this has not all been the most colossal waste of time?'

There's a long silence. The Quiet Gentleman dips a cloth into a bowl of water and very deliberately wipes the dust off his face before he speaks. 'It was never a promise and you never told me about the guards,' he says.

'You didn't think there'd be security?'

'Between here and the mountains is half a day's walk. You can't do it in the daylight or you'll get spotted and you can't do it at night because there are patrols.'

'And you think I'd hide that from you?' Thutmose's

voice is grating, but he sounds rattled.

'I don't know what you would hide from me. And things weren't much better when we got into the mountains.' The Quiet Gentleman pauses. 'Did you know about the town?'

'Town? It's a prison camp.'

'It's a town. It may be guarded and it may be impossible to get in or out, but it's no prison. Every morning we saw a long line of people marching out and every evening we saw them coming back, and you know what they were?'

'Prisoners,' Thutmose snaps.

'Builders. Foreign builders. They had a northern look about them. I'll bet my reputation on it.'

'Impossible! I provide the builders for the royal household. Where were they going?'

'Couldn't say. We couldn't get close enough. It's guarded morning, noon and night. That's how Menna got injured. We tried to get nearer at night and the guards put an arrow in him. Luckily it was dark and the guards thought they'd hit an animal. We were close enough to hear exactly who thought it was a lion and who thought it was a dog.'

'And you think this town in the desert might have something to do with our . . . quarry?' Thutmose sounds interested.

'I think it's got everything to do with it,' the Quiet Gentleman says. 'I'd bet my reputation on it and it shows just how little you are valued by the palace. But that's not the point and we both know it. You need another plan and I've got it, but we have to change the terms of our agreement.'

This gets Thutmose angry. 'A bold fellow. A very bold fellow indeed. You come to me like a beggar and try to dictate terms?'

'I was never a beggar and I'm not dictating anything. Your way has failed; now we try mine. Take it or leave it, but if you take it, it's on my terms,' the Quiet Gentleman says.

His voice is level and calm and the 'take it or leave it' note makes me squirm. He shouldn't be talking like this because when Thutmose finds out that the Quiet Gentleman isn't Jatty, he'll go mad.

Thutmose inhales. His head pecks to the left and the right and suddenly he looks like an old man with a lot of problems. I almost feel sorry for him as he hobbles out.

23. In which the Quiet Gentleman puts me straight

The Quiet Gentleman raises an eyebrow when I stand and show myself. For the first time ever he looks something other than calm and impassive. Folds run from his nostrils to the corners of his mouth and there are dark shadows under his eyes. He's thinner too.

'So,' he says. 'Managed to stay out of trouble?'

'I think so,' I say.

'And did any of that make sense to you?'

'It makes no sense at all,' I say. 'Why would anyone shoot arrows at you for trying to find a quarry?'

He blinks at me wearily. 'I can't be bothered to explain,' he says. 'Have they been keeping you busy?'

'Working on the gypsum.'

'You won't be doing that much longer.'

'I won't be doing anything. We've got to get out of here right now! The man in charge of firing the rocks knows the real Jatty. He owes . . . owed him money.'

The Quiet Gentleman goes very still. 'And you decided to warn me?' he says.

'Of course. You said we were in this together,' I protest, outraged.

'I said that because it suited me. You . . . oh, never mind. I need to think.'

'But we don't have time!' I say. 'And I'm going mad and Imi's just . . . she's not herself. I feel like she's disappearing.'

'If we run now, we'll throw everything away.' The Quiet Gentleman's big face has smoothed out now and his dark eyes glow. 'Listen hard, mud boy. There's a new edict: you can't leave the city without a pass, and even if we sneaked on to the dockside, there's not a captain in the Two Kingdoms who'd risk his neck to carry us away. Of course there's always the desert if you fancy dying of thirst or being picked up by one of the king's patrols.

'And suppose you do get back home? Those people you call your parents will have got themselves another potboy and you'll be out on your ear. There's no going back. We have to think about the future. If I'm going to be found out, there's no gain in waiting for someone else to do it. But if you tell Thutmose, that puts you in the right. Yes, it might be enough to jolt him into action. He's spent two years staring at that unfinished sculpture of the queen's head and doing nothing. He needs a fire lit underneath him.'

'What are you talking about? What's the head got to do with anything?'

'You'll find out. Now, you run to Thutmose and you betray me, boy. That'll get you off the hook and then at least one of us is safe. Understand?'

'Yes, but . . .'

'But what?'

The words are in my mind and I can't stop them bursting out of my mouth. 'What about you?'

He raises his eyes to the heavens, but this time seems almost amused.

'I can look after myself, boy. Just do what I say.'

So nervous I feel sick, I run to Thutmose to give the Quiet Gentleman up.

He's standing with Scarface by the table and I start off

by throwing myself on the ground and begging him to protect me, calling him the jewel of the Two Kingdoms, the blessing of the river, the son of the blackest mud – all the things I heard my father say when he wanted to suck up to an important guest. I say that my tongue may wither at my news, and my mouth fill with dust, but what I know weighs so heavy on my heart that I'm frightened it may break the scales of the divine Ma'at (I forget that Ma'at, the goddess who weighs our souls when we die, has been banned like all the others), BUT (taking a deep breath), BUT (and another one), I have evidence that he is harbouring a traitor in his midst, a serpent, a worm, a liar and a murderer.

And then I shout: 'It's Jatty, or the man who calls himself Jatty!'

'Jatty!' Scarface snarls. 'I told you there was something wrong about him.'

'Quiet!' Thutmose's voice cuts across the general thuggish muttering in the room. 'What do you mean, "or the man who calls himself Jatty"?'

So I tell them about the murder on the boat and add in a bit about the Quiet Gentleman laughing a blood-curdling laugh as the crocodiles tore into the real Jatty's poor corpse. Then I throw myself on to my face again and wait while angry voices rage above my head. When the storm settles, I peer up and see that Thutmose is looking down at me.

'Indeed,' he says. 'Indeed. And do you have any idea what this imposter wants?'

'No, master,' I whine. 'But I think he has a plan.'

Thutmose thinks. 'You: go and fetch him.' He nods to three of his heavies. 'You: stay here.' He nods at me.

Very soon, there's a commotion in the corridor that grows louder and louder. Finally the Quiet Gentleman is brought in, straining against his captors, one of whom has a black eye, another a swelling nose and the third with a split lip.

'Well, indeed, well, indeed, indeed,' Thutmose says. 'Brother Jatty appears instead to be Brother Who Isn't Jatty, and according to my young friend here, we have been hiding a fugitive from justice in our precious home. Do you know how they punish murderers here?'

'I don't know what you're talking about,' the Quiet Gentleman says sullenly.

'So you are Jatty?'

'And who says I'm not?' He looks around and pretends to notice me for the first time. 'You? You've been spreading your lies? I'll wear your guts for a necklace! I'll twist your head round on its scrawny neck! I'll chew the skin off your fingers and crunch the bones!'

He lunges at me, dragging the two men who are hanging on to his arms with him. He only stops when the third pulls out a knife and jams it against his neck.

'Very interesting,' Thutmose says. 'And so poetic.

Are you saying this child is a liar?'

'There's a man up at the ovens who knows the real Jatty,' I gabble. 'Fetch him.'

'Hmm. All in good time. You see, what intrigues me is that you waited until now to share this with us,' Thutmose says. 'Now, why would that be? Wouldn't it have been easier to tell me when he was away?'

I hadn't thought of that. I throw myself back down on to my face and stammer: 'Yes, master. It wasn't until he came back that I realised how much I hated him for what he had done.'

Thutmose narrows his eyes, then sends a messenger to the beehive ovens.

To keep up appearances, the Quiet Gentleman is staring at me in the same way he used to at the inn. It takes me back to the time before he arrived, and when I think of how simple and straightforward and relatively trouble-free my life was then, I start to snivel a bit.

Anyway, the man from the kilns comes and sure enough, when Thutmose asks him if his old friend Jatty is in the room, he looks around and just says: 'Where?'

That does it. All the men start shouting, although none of them could have known Jatty, and carry on until Thutmose lifts a hand to silence them.

'Gentlemen, gentlemen,' he says. 'We're not going to find out about our friend's plan if you kill him, are we? No, indeed. Now this plan must be a good one or Brother

Who Isn't Jatty wouldn't have taken such ridiculous risks. Am I right?'

'It's a good plan,' the Quiet Gentleman says. 'But if you want to know what it is, we'll have to talk in private.'

'We speak with my men here or not all,' Thutmose says.

And the Quiet Gentleman shrugs and looks resigned. I can see the fools guarding him relax. I brace myself.

Suddenly one of them is on the ground, another is bent double and making a funny whistling noise, and the one that was holding the knife is looking at his empty hand and holding his wrist, which is crooked. There's a moment of complete and utter stillness, broken only by the clatter of that knife hitting the flagstone floor and Thutmose's shocked bleat as he finds the Quiet Gentleman standing behind him with a very large arm around his throat.

'I never came to hurt you, Thutmose, because I need your help,' the Quiet Gentleman says. 'But I'm not going to share my plan with anyone other than you. I never took you for a fool, but as things stand, I'm beginning to wonder if your reputation hasn't gone to your head a little.'

'My reputation can take care of itself,' Thutmose answers calmly enough. 'I care nothing for it, or yours for that matter. The question is not what a man has done yesterday, but what he can do tomorrow. But if it means so much to you, we can talk in private.'

He waves his men away to the far corners of the big

room and the Quiet Gentleman lets him go. Thutmose takes a deep breath, then relaxes.

'Say your piece,' he says.

'I know what you really want,' the Quiet Gentleman says. 'I know looking in the mountains for a new . . . quarry was always a fool's mission. I know that the best way, the only way to get what you want is to put someone inside the palace. Someone you can rely on.'

'Guess away, Brother Who Is Not Jatty. Just tell me what your so-called plan is,' Thutmose says.

'The boy I brought with me is the key,' the Quiet Gentleman says. 'The first thing you must do is let him prove his worth.'

My first reaction is to think, *Me? He's talking about me?* My second is to swell up with pride, like a pond frog in spring. My third is to wonder what they mean by getting into the palace.

'He can stick at a task, I grant you,' Thutmose said. 'But then so can a donkey if you hit it often enough.'

'He's no donkey,' the Quiet Gentleman says, his voice very level. 'We'll look at your model of the queen's head and talk more in the morning.'

'The head?' Thutmose tilts his head on one side. 'The head?'

The Quiet Gentleman yawns and stretches. 'We'll talk in the morning,' he says.

The silence grows tenser and tenser as it stretches out.

Then Thutmose shakes his head.

'You'll sleep here,' he says. 'The boy goes back to the workshops. I'll not have you trying to escape with him.'

'Why would we want to escape, master craftsman, when we are so close to our goal?' the Quiet Gentleman says, and I realise that he's won the battle and, for the time being, I'm safe.

24. In which I understand an idea

I'm sent for first thing in the morning. The Quiet Gentleman is waiting for me in Thutmose's courtyard, a huge breakfast laid out in front of him. He waves a goose leg at me.

'Eaten?' he asks. 'Had a good night's sleep?'

I shake my head. 'How could I? The wounded man was raving all night. Wouldn't shut up.'

'And what was he talking about?'

'The sun. How he was going to steal it.' I watch his reaction.

All he says is: 'And what did you think of that?'

'Nonsense. Except it was what you said to me on the boat. None of it makes sense. I didn't understand what you were talking about then and I'm no clearer now.'

'Let's take one thing at a time,' the Quiet Gentleman

says. 'The queen's head that's on a bench in Thutmose's studio – try some honey cake. No? – I think you can finish it.'

'What? The honey cake?'

'No. The queen's head.'

'You're mad,' I say. 'Crazy. That time you spent in the desert has addled your brain. You got a knock on the head. Admit it.'

He picks a bit of goose flesh from between his teeth. 'I've seen you work with mud,' he says. 'You can easily learn how to work with gypsum. You finish off the queen's head and that gets you into the palace.'

'Why do I want to get into the palace?'

'One thing at a time. The queen's head. How about it?'

'I can't do that,' I stammer. 'I make animals.'

'You made a model of my head back at the inn.'

'But that was just . . . I did it because I was angry with you. The animals I make, they're good, but it's like the mud is talking to me. I don't have to think about it. When I do a person, I have to see them.'

'Listen, boy. I've seen you at work and yes, it's like the mud talks to you and you talk to it. I've heard you chant that rhyme and I know it's about the old gods. But I also know this place is different. The king isn't a god and neither is the queen. They're just people.'

'But I don't know what she looks like!'

'Is that your only objection?'

100

'It's quite a big one!'

His face splits into a smile. 'Then we're in luck. Every week, the king and queen appear at a palace window to be seen by the people – it's one of his new ideas – and they throw gifts and money down. If you got close, you'd be able to see enough of the queen to bring the model of her head on a bit.'

'When?'

'Now. This morning.'

'But I've never done anything like it,' I say. 'It's too much to ask.'

'That's the end of it then. End of you. End of Imi. End of those miserable creatures you call your parents. End of me.'

'So no pressure then.'

'Pressure is all in the mind. What's the worst thing that can happen?'

I shake my head. 'I don't know.'

'So it's settled. Now eat. I want you fresh. Alert. Clever.'

'I want Imi to come too,' I say. 'If she gets nothing else out of being dragged away from her home, I want her to see the king and queen.'

He nods slowly.

Half an hour later, we leave the workshops and set off: Imi, the Quiet Gentleman and me.

At first the street outside the workshops is empty, but soon we meet other people walking in the same direction as us. That street feeds into a bigger one and now all the little groups have become a crowd. Then we enter another street full of people and our crowd sort of folds itself into their crowd, and then that big crowd meets another bigger crowd, and another and another, all heading for the Royal Road which runs between the king's palace and the queen's palace. There's a bridge connecting the palaces and it's on this bridge that the king is due to appear with this wife, the beautiful Nefertiti.

Before I know it, I'm wedged between two people, I can't see a thing and the only way to move is by taking quick, shuffling steps. If I fall, I'll be trampled underfoot. Imi and the Quiet Gentleman have disappeared and no way am I going to get a glimpse of the queen from here. I've got to do something about it.

I start to shove myself sideways and people are jammed together so tightly there's nothing they can do. My face gets mushed into body parts I'd rather avoid, but eventually I'm at the edge of the crowd, except now I'm being ground against the whitewashed wall of the palace.

The plasterwork is so rough it gives me an idea. Bracing myself against a young man, I scrabble up the wall until I'm high enough to sit on the ledge of a high window and really see what's going on.

The Royal Road is wide. The bridge is covered but has a big, square window in the middle of it. Crowds have approached from both ends of the street and people are packed so tightly that the tops of their heads look like cobblestones.

Imi's about twenty paces away, perched on the Quiet Gentleman's shoulders. He is tall enough to see over everyone's heads and he's looking around for me. I wave; he sees me and nods up at the window on the covered bridge. Everyone is craning forward so that now the street is like a river of upturned faces. A sighing noise rises from it like mist.

I stare and stare at the empty window until dark dots dance in front of my eyes, and then I see a figure. But it's not the king and it's not the queen. It's a girl.

The crowd cheers, but I feel as if I've been blasted by lightning.

I'm struck dumb. I can't breathe. I've never seen anyone or anything so perfect. She looks down at the crowd, her eyes lit up with an emotion that I can't read, but she looks so alive, so . . . so free.

She goes. There's a moment's silence, then another face appears and the crowd cheers even more loudly.

This is clearly Queen Nefertiti. With her long neck, narrow jaw, fine cheekbones and huge slanting eyes, her beauty is as different from the princess's as the moon is from the sun. Her high crown is topped with a sacred cobra and, as she moves her head, the snake seems to nod along with her. There is no expression on her face, no expression at all. It's as if she's already been modelled in

Thutmose's workshop. A perfect mask.

She reaches her hand out of the window and coins drop from it, glinting.

Gold! The crowd seethes. I see Imi lurch as the Quiet Gentleman almost loses his footing, but then he's steady again. Now the street is like a field, raised arms waving like wheat in the breeze, hands reaching upwards, hoping for a touch of the coins.

The queen steps back and the king appears. His size is a shock after the princess and queen. He is tall and his shoulders fill the window. His face seems huge with dark eyes, flared nostrils and full, wide lips. The queen looked tense, but he just looks still, like water in a well.

He raises a hand. More gold flies from his fingers, but there's a disturbance in the crowd about twenty paces away. Someone very small is jumping up and down, and when I look more closely, I see that it's Sethi. I beckon, but just as he starts to push his way towards me, the king retreats into the palace and everything changes.

The crowd on my side of the bridge is trying to push on, but so is the crowd on the other side. No one's actually moving, but surges and currents run through the packed mass like swirls in the Great River. A woman falls; a big man stumbles over her and grabs at another man, pulling him down and also a woman who was leaning against him. Suddenly it's chaos and Sethi disappears.

I move before I think. I know that the crowd is packed

so tightly that someone as light as me can run across shoulders and heads without falling through and, what's more, no one has the space to push me away. So I swing down from the window, stumble across the uneven floor of people, and when I get to the spot where I think I saw Sethi, I dive down, like a duck.

He's there on the ground – I can just part the waves of flesh enough to see him. I yell his name and he looks up, sees my face and stretches out a hand. I grab it. I've nearly got him upright when there's another one of those uncontrollable crowd surges and we're pulled apart, and then I'm falling. I find myself next to Sethi in a forest of legs and then suddenly a gap opens up around us. We get to our feet, hang on to each other and allow ourselves to be pulled and pushed and tossed and turned along with the crowd.

Now we're under the bridge, now the squeeze is lessening, and now we're running, me and Sethi, in the same direction as everyone else down the long road. We leave the palace behind us, then the grand houses and then we're out into the glaring desert and I'm staring at the strangest building I have ever seen.

25. In which an idea bears fruit

'What is that?' I ask.

I'm buffeted as people run past us, heading to what look like giant pillars guarding a massive walled enclosure. It glares white and is as big as town, as big as a city.

'That's the Great Temple, stupid,' Sethi says. Now I remember seeing it from the boat, but had no idea it was so big. 'Haven't you ever seen a temple before?'

'The ones back home are like dark halls with huge pillars. They're not open like this.'

'That's so the sun god can see everything inside,' Sethi says. 'Anyway, we'd better hurry.'

The gate towers rear up like mountains, red banners hanging limply in the heat. Clustered around their base is a small village of bakeries. I smell woodsmoke and bread, and my mouth begins to water, but Sethi is running again.

'Come on!'

The high gates to the temple are closed, but the crowd is already bunching up around them. Sethi leads me past and turns right up the far side of the temple, heading for a cattle pen made of rough mud bricks. He waves an arm towards it and winks.

'That's our way in.'

I boost him up on to the wall, then he gives me a hand

to scrabble up next to him. We're looking down on a solid mass of terrified cattle, eyes rolling, tongues hanging out, streaming with spit. The slaves are picking them out, washing them, then beating and prodding them one by one into a tunnel that bores straight through the temple wall.

'What's going on?' I ask.

'Sacrifices. They kill the cows in the temple and lay them out on tables as offerings for the sun god.'

'And why are we here?'

'To sneak in.'

'To watch cows being killed?'

'No, stupid. It's not just meat that's offered up. There's bread and fruit and beer – everything you want to eat and drink – all laid out. The king blesses it, offers it to the sun and then they open the gates and everyone in the city rushes in to grab what they can. But if we get there first, we can eat and drink ourselves silly in peace and we won't have to fight with anyone. It gets messy, I can tell you. Quick! Now! We can go now!'

A panicking cow has knocked a slave over and everyone in the pen is concentrating on that. Sethi drops down into the enclosure and sprints into the tunnel. I follow.

The temple wall is maybe ten paces thick. Sethi is waiting at the far end by a gate of stout timbers, but with big enough gaps between them to squeeze through. I follow – what else can I do? – and stand blinking for a second in the fierce sun. The light in the temple is blinding: the whole area, as big as a city, is glaring white. I glimpse busy, half-naked men, dead cows, blood . . .

Immediately to the right there's a great stack of timber that we dive behind. It's not a moment too soon. There's a crash behind us as the gate is pushed back and a bellowing cow is led into the temple.

From behind the woodstack we watch a priest step up and bless it, then hurriedly step back as a gigantic man, naked apart from a bloodstained loincloth, swings an axe into the cow's neck. The noise it makes is heavy and wet. The cow goes down and immediately men with hooks, half a dozen of them, drag it away to a sort of scaffold where it's hoisted up by its back legs and butchered.

Sethi is anxious to press on and now my eyes have adjusted I can make out the rest of the temple.

I'm looking at a vast court. There are two big, square buildings in it, a large one in the middle and a smaller one right at the end. Near the gate closest to the city stand rows of short, square blocks, each one about my height. There are hundreds of them, too many to count, laid out in straight rows, all piled with food.

'What are we doing?' I whisper to Sethi.

He points at the blocks.

'All that food,' he says. 'It's just for me and you.'

26. In which I have an unexpected encounter

Empty carts pull up at the woodpile with a creaking of wheels. When Sethi starts to help load the timber from the stack, I join in. I can see his plan now. The timber is for the fire altar that stands in front of the temple's main building. The fire's already been lit and the wood is so dry it burns without smoke and the building seems to dance in the invisible, lethal heat.

When the carts are piled high with wood, we walk with it, just a couple more skinny slaves with badly shaved heads and dirty tunics. Close to the fire altar we break away and hide again, keeping close to the wall and out of sight of the few priests.

'What now?' I whisper. Anyone can see us from the back of the temple. The only other place to hide is in among the offering tables, but between them and us there's a lot of empty sand. There's no way we can cross it without being seen.

'When the king arrives at the gate, all the priests go and welcome him. That's when we run for the offering tables. The ones on the left have the fruit and bread and drink – the ones on the right are for the meat.'

'But we'll be seen,' I say.

He doesn't say anything, and if he did I wouldn't have

heard because a monstrous roar of horns and a thousand clashing bells drown out all thought. I put my hands over my ears, but Sethi is peering round the edge of the sanctuary and then he's running across the dazzling white expanse towards the offering tables and I'm following.

We throw ourselves down behind the first table we come to, then scuttle along the rows until we're hidden. The tables are so closely packed together that the only way we could be seen is if someone looks down the row we're in. And Sethi's right. They're piled high with food: loaves of bread, mountains of fruit, stacks of vegetables, ranks of tall jars, all lying under the merciless, hungry, golden eye of the sun.

Sethi stops when we get to the tables with the big jars on them.

'Beer,' he says, his face lit up and happy. 'Come on. Help me!'

The jugs are too heavy for one person to handle; you need one person to tip and the other to stand under the stream of alcohol with his mouth open. It looks so good and I'm thirsty . . . but the beer is thin and sour. We would never have served this in the inn, not that Sethi minds. He drinks again and when I have another it doesn't seem so bad after all. A memory swims into my mind of the Quiet Gentleman sitting on a bench in the inn, beer by his side, eyes closed against the sun. For a second I wonder where he is, and where Imi is too, then have another drink. I feel dizzy and ravenously hungry now. We crawl back towards the tables with food on them. We don't check the rows as carefully as we did before, but why should we worry? Who's going to be looking for us?

We split a loaf between us and stuff it with tomatoes and onions. It's the best food I've ever eaten. The tomatoes are juicy, the onions are sweet and the bread is soft, still warm from the bakery.

In the distance, music starts again. Horns and bells and then the wail of strings. I'm happy just sitting with my back against an offering table, sun on one side, shade on the other.

'Come on. I want figs,' Sethi says.

I stick my head up to look at the offering tables. One of them must have figs on it. I can see that the fire altar is billowing black smoke now because they're cooking the meat, and the smell of roasting drifts over the air. My mouth starts to water. I feel great and, even if the world is spinning round ever so slightly, this is getting on for the best day I've ever had.

We scurry off on all fours. We find wheat, more bread, mutton and piles of fish that's already spoiling and black with flies. And then we see the fruit: a soft pyramid of purple figs, their skins soft and splitting. I can almost feel the squishiness of the pulp and the crunch the tiny seeds. I lose all caution and move forward, and it's not until I'm almost there that I hear voices. Adult voices.

111

My excitement collapses into panic. I look behind me. No Sethi. Where is he? I flatten myself behind the nearest table and try to work out where the voices came from. I've completely forgotten about the figs. All I can think about is the trouble I'm in.

I hear the voices again. They're chattering, arguing even, and as they get closer to me, I can make out what they're saying. A woman is complaining in a high, haughty voice that the arrangements were not satisfactory AGAIN and the princess is not to show herself at the Window of Appearances at any price.

A girl laughs.

Princess?

'Meritaten, no! You know they're not for you!'

'But the sun god wouldn't mind, Mother,' a girl laughs. 'Anyway, Daddy could ask him for me.'

'Don't bother your father. And that sounds like blasphemy.'

Mother. Father. Meritaten. King. Queen. Princess. If my heart was thumping before, it's beating flat out now. I'm stuck in the temple, where I know I shouldn't be, and I'm eavesdropping on a conversation between the queen and the princess. If I'm seen, I'll be killed. Terror is a hand around my throat. I've got to move, and quickly too.

Carefully, I peer out. To the left, nothing. Right then. A quick glimpse is enough. She's there, about ten paces away: the princess I saw at the window. I can see the jewels glinting on the straps of her little sandals; I can see the dust on her feet.

Then I see the queen. She is tall and slender. She's wearing a long, white, pleated dress that clings to her body and the towering crown looks heavy. There is sweat on her forehead. There are two little frown lines between her eyes. I can see the hollow of her cheeks and her mouth is down at the corners. I stare and stare and stare, trying to press the image of her face into my mind. The unfinished sculpture in Thutmose's workshop was like a promise of beauty, but now I see her I realise that he could only capture the mask she wears in public. What I am seeing now is different. More interesting. More real. But she is really, really close.

I edge away, working my way around one altar and then another. Finally I move back directly away from them, peering down the rows as I go.

There's Sethi. He's got his back to me.

'Psst.'

He looks round, sees me and starts to crawl. He's not being very cautious. I wave at him frantically to slow down, but he just ploughs on.

There's a shout! Sethi's been seen! He leaps up and runs towards me. I'm horrified and try to shoo him away, but it's no good. I scuttle off, keeping as low as I can. I know he's following. I can hear the guards and the princess, whose shrill, excited voice rises above everyone else's.

'Thief! A thief! He's stealing from the god! Stop him!'

The guards are blocking the way back to the cattle pen. The sun stares down at us mercilessly as if to say: you're in my temple, you've stolen my food, of course you cannot escape.

In a sick panic I double back. There's a bad moment when I see a guard coming towards me, but he's looking to the side and I dart across the passageway, jink to the right, straighten up, jink left. Sethi's caught up now and we're heading towards the back of the temple; the hunt is getting further away from us as they head to the front.

We stop to catch our breath. Sethi collapses beside me.

'How do we get out?' I say. He looks at me, blankly. 'What did you do last time?' I press.

'I just waited until they opened the gates and let the crowd in.'

'That's the plan?' I'm horrified. Before we can argue, a voice silences us.

'I can see you!' It is light and mocking.

We stare wildly around. Sethi panics and sticks his head up.

'Aha! Now I really can see you. Stay there or I'll scream!'

The voice is coming from my left. I crawl right. It sounds like the princess, but she's only seen Sethi so I keep going.

'I can hear another one!'

I try the trick I did before, of doubling back on my tracks.

114

'Where are you?'

The voice is a bit further away now. Has it worked? I'm moving as quickly as I can, checking the rows as I go . . .

'Got you!'

Checking in all directions except behind me.

'Stop or I'll scream! I mean it.'

I stop.

I turn.

And I stare.

The princess is every bit as beautiful as when I saw her in the window. I can see now that she's about my height, but slender rather than scrawny. Her skin is smooth, her eyes are dark and her hair oiled and glossy. It's been plaited into ringlets and shimmers when she turns her head. Her lips are turned up in a little smile.

Blood and breath are roaring in my ears and I can't seem to move. She takes a step towards me.

'Do you know how I caught you?' she says.

She squats down so she's on a level with me, like I'm a strange animal to be peered at. I dare to shake my head. She points up at the sun.

'Do you think it's just my father who can speak to him? He's a god and so am I. I just asked the Aten.'

'The A-A-Aten?'

'The s-s-s-sun. That hot old thing up in the sky.'

I believe her. I dare to nod. She laughs.

'Idiot. Did you think I'd ask the Aten for that? Do you

115

think I'd waste my breath and his time? Any old fool could work out what you were going to do. You did it twice. All the others are crashing off in the wrong direction. Who's your friend?'

'S-S-Sethi.'

'And what's your name?'

'I don't really have one. They just call me boy.'

'Boy! Hah! Do you want to know my name?'

I nod. It seems to be expected.

'Daughter-of-the-King's-Body-His-Beloved-Daughter-Meritaten-Born-of-the-Great-Royal-Wife-His-Gracious-Lady-Queen-of-the-Two-Kingdoms-May-She-Live-Forever,' she recites. 'What do you think of that?'

'Very . . . noble,' I say.

She makes a rubbery sound with her lips. 'Very stupid. Why should my mother live forever? She's trying to stop me getting married. I wish she'd die. What are you doing here?'

I'm relieved she asked me that because I don't know how to answer anything else.

'We wanted figs.' It sounds so stupid, but it was the right thing to say.

The princess opens her eyes wide. 'I wanted figs too.' She frowns. 'Unless you're just saying that because you heard me.'

I shake my head. 'No. We had bread and tomatoes and beer and then we wanted figs.'

'Beer! I've never had beer and my mother says I'm too young for wine.'

'The beer's not good. It's not ready to drink yet.'

'That's blasphemy. The Aten wants the best. I shall tell the king and the priests shall be punished. Someone will die, I expect. Do you still want figs?'

I nod.

'Here.'

She reaches out to one of the offering tables, picks a fig and throws it at my head. It's a good shot. I manage to turn my face so it explodes on my ear. The princess bursts out laughing. I pick ripe fig out of my ear and flick it on to the ground.

'Not very grateful,' the princess says, 'throwing the god's food away like that. How shall I punish you?'

In the distance I hear voices calling. 'Meritaten! Meritaten!'

'That's my nurse. I have to go,' she says. 'The question is, do I turn you in or do I show mercy?'

I take a huge breath. 'The Aten has seen me,' I say. 'He will punish me if he thinks fit.'

'Clever boy, boy, but I think you might be too insignificant for the Aten to notice, so it'll be up to me to mete out punishment. The trouble is I almost feel sorry for you. How do I check to make sure you've not been bad again?'

'If someone as great and powerful as you calls, I will come,' I try.

'That's amusing,' she said. She sucks her teeth. 'And you've sort of been clever again. It's flattery designed to get you off the hook. Perhaps you're too clever. Hmm. Tell me where you live and I might let you go.'

'W-Where I live?'

'You have to live somewhere. Come on. Or I scream for help RIGHT NOW.'

'At the workshops of Thutmose,' I gabble.

'What? Thutmose the master craftsman? That old stick? He's in big trouble with my father. Or maybe my mother. Anyway, he blew it.'

I nod miserably, angry with myself for not being able to think of a lie.

'All right. Any time I want, I can send my soldiers to find you. Yes. I like the idea of that. And don't even think of running away or I shall order them to slaughter Thutmose and everyone else in his workshops until you're found.'

She turns and runs off, her light feet pattering on the packed sand of the temple floor.

'They went that way,' I hear her call. 'There were two of them. Two ugly, skinny, dirty, worthless little thieving city rats.'

She's waving towards the other end of the field of altars and the guards go thundering off. I take a deep breath and collapse. That was the most frightening experience of my life, but I've only bought us a bit of time.

118

The princess has seen me and she knows where I live.

Sethi finds me and our ordeal doesn't last much longer. The sun has only moved a finger's breadth across the sky before we hear a noise like a stampede of cattle and the hard, packed sand of the temple floor starts to drum.

'Sit tight,' Sethi says.

'What is it?'

'Wait for it, wait for it, wait for it . . . Now look. They've opened the gates.'

It's like a dam breaking. People are sprinting across the temple floor and in among the offering tables, grabbing this, grabbing that, fighting over flyblown sides of meat, huge stinking fish, piles of wilting vegetables.

We wait. A wind gets up, sweeping into the temple from the desert. It's hot and hard and spits grit into my eyes, on to my skin, coating the food offerings.

In front of me, two men fight over a melon until it splits in half with a rotten crack and they both tumble to the floor. The wind blows harder. The dust is making it difficult to see. People are wrapping their clothes around their mouths as Sethi and I finally stagger off towards the main gate.

As we walk down the Royal Road back to the workshops, I try to make sense of what I've seen. The smell of blood and fear and rot still lingers and I can't shift the images from my mind. All that blood spilled. All that life gone, but where? Does the sun take it up in the same way it sucks up a puddle of water? Is the heat of the day the god's long, hot, endless breath?

But it doesn't matter. I've seen the queen – and not just a snatched glimpse through a high window. And, stranger than strange, I've talked to the princess.

27. In which I prove my worth

The next morning, the Quiet Gentleman pulls me out of the crushing yard before I've started work. He puts his heavy hands on my shoulders and looks into my face.

'I hope you managed to get a good look at the queen yesterday,' he says. 'Lost you in the crowd.'

'Better than you think,' I say.

'And you're ready for the task?'

'I don't know,' I say.

'You'd better be, because now is the time to prove your worth. It's not just your safety we're talking about. It's your sister's too. Remember: because this plan is mine, Thutmose might try to mess it up. But everything is riding on it for us.'

I swallow nervously and follow him to the workshops, hoping my hand will stop trembling and the butterflies in my stomach will stop fluttering.

Thutmose is waiting. The cloth has been pulled from

the queen's head and I look at it. I mean, really look at it. Now I have a picture of her in my head, I can see where Thutmose has gone wrong. As well as it not having any personality, her forehead is too low below the towering crown and there's something wrong with the eyes.

I touch my own cheekbone and feel the way the skin slides on bone under the pressure of my fingers. I touch the sculpture; the smooth blur of the soft white stone can be my guide, like the skull beneath the skin. I put both hands on the queen's head, close my eyes and call up the image of her face: not the still mask I glimpsed in the Window of Appearances, but the worried mother I saw in the temple. I feel my fingers move.

I blink my eyes open. Thutmose hunches forward, watching me like a crow.

A bowl of plaster and a range of tools I've never seen before have been placed on the workbench: small trowels, big trowels, scrapers, knives. I've never used anything like them, but perhaps they'll come in useful later. My fingers dance in the bowl of white gypsum, feeling its texture, its weight. Then nothing. Just silence that seems like a question.

What is she?

She is . . . I think. She is what? A queen? Yes. That's what everyone sees, but she is also someone else. She is also herself.

When I made animals, I wasn't making a particular cow

121

or bird, I was making every cow, every bird. This is different. This is about the *I am* and the *She is*. This is about showing the difference that makes each of us who we are.

'She is,' I say out loud. 'She is.'

I am ready. I take some of the plaster and press it on to the cheekbone. I have to think of the whole head – there's a gentle double curve that runs from the top of the eye, over the cheek and then round until it disappears into the jaw. And then I have to do the other side. Next I have to make the lips a bit fuller. Good. But now, now I have to find the right expression.

I close my eyes again and summon up the two images of her that I have: one on the bridge and the other in the temple. Two faces, both her. The one smiling like a queen; the other frowning like a mother. But suppose she frowns like a queen and smiles like a mother. Does that mean she has four faces?

No.

It's the same face, but while hers can change, the one I am making can't. All those expressions have to live in the hardness of the stone, in the curve of the plaster. One face, one person, one expression that says: I am a queen and I am everything else.

That's good. With my head thinking the right thoughts, my hands can do the right thing. I see that I was wrong about the forehead, but I don't quite know how until I give the eyebrows a bit more of an arch and imagine them painted as the queen's were, and then it's better.

I work. I close my eyes to remember and work again. Then I hear someone talking to me and I realise they've been doing so for some time.

'It's time to rest now. It's time to rest.' I look up. It's Thutmose, but his voice is unusually gentle. My neck aches in the way it used to when I was working the potter's wheel all day. My legs are tired. I have a cramp in my hands that I can only relieve by flexing my fingers.

'I can take it from here,' Thutmose says. 'You've done quite enough. Yes, indeed. Extraordinary. Quite extraordinary.' He sounds almost kind.

28. In which I learn my fate

I wake up the next morning and wander into the workshop, rubbing my eyes and yawning.

The Quiet Gentleman and Thutmose are there. Thutmose has lifted the head and the Quiet Gentleman seems to be examining its base. They're talking about something technical.

'So that's why the neck's so long,' the Quiet Gentleman is saying. 'The stuff goes in and plans come out . . .'

But Thutmose clears his throat noisily and nods towards me. The Quiet Gentleman turns. I think he's hiding something in his palm, but I can't see what it is, and anyway, all thoughts are blown away when I see what has been done to my work.

The queen I left was as white as flour. Overnight she has been painted. Her skin is the colour of skin, and her eyes are gems the colour of her eyes. The Quiet Gentleman bows in mock humility.

'And now it is time to show it,' he says.

'Imi first,' I say.

Imi is led in by the cook. When she sees the head, she claps her hands and smiles a real smile.

'It's all for you,' I whisper in her ear.

'No,' she says, as the cook pretends to faint because it looks so real, 'it's for you.'

All through the morning, visitors come to see the head, one by one at first and then a steady stream. Women wearing costly gems and men dripping in gold admire it, congratulate Thutmose and say he has done what no other craftsman has ever managed. The Quiet Gentleman whispers in my ear that I shouldn't worry because Thutmose won't dare go anywhere without me now. But the really important thing is this: with so many people seeing it, news will get back to the palace in no time at all. Thutmose will be summoned to bring the sculpture and he will have to take me with him.

My stomach tightens into a knot. 'But . . .'

The Quiet Gentleman takes me out into an empty yard and squats with his back to the wall so we can see who is coming. 'Your job is only half done,' he says in a low voice. 'We need someone on the inside of the palace.'

'Inside the palace? But why? And don't talk in riddles about stealing the sun. I needed to see the queen to make her head; I need to know your plan to make it work too,' I answer.

He turns his head towards me and looks at me blankly. 'What am I?' he asks wearily. 'You know it so you may as well say it.'

'A tomb robber.' My voice is tiny.

'Louder.'

'A tomb robber.'

'So what was I looking for in the desert? And don't pretend you think I was looking for a quarry.'

'For tombs?'

'Think! This city has only just been built. The only people who've died so far are slaves and paupers – nothing to steal there.'

I shake my head dumbly.

'I was looking for the king's tomb, you little idiot,' he says. 'We weren't even sure he would have one and we're still not, but that secret town in the desert I stumbled on is the biggest clue yet. Trouble is, it's too heavily guarded to get close.'

'So what have I got to do with any of this?'

'There will be plans and maps inside the palace. The problem is getting anything in or out. The king's so frightened of spies, assassins, plague, priests that the whole place has been shut down and security is very tight. That's where you come in.

'By now the palace will have heard about the head. Next, Thutmose will be invited in to present it but he'll take you in case he actually has to do something to the head on the spot. But that's only half the job. When you're inside, Thutmose's contact will hand over the plans for the tomb. That's when you have to say that something needs doing to the head – it doesn't matter what – but it can only be done in the workshops. You bring the head out with the plans and . . . job done.'

It's like I'm in a bubble. I feel like I'm floating. I can't hear anything for a while except for the blood roaring in my ears.

'You're making me a tomb robber?' My voice seems to be coming from outside the bubble. It's very thin and distant.

'As soon as we set sail for the city, you were a tomb robber,' the Quiet Gentleman says. 'No turning back now.'

'If I say no?'

'I'll snap your neck right now then go and do the same to your sister. Less time you live, less time you have to blab. Don't make me. This is the path you're on.'

'But . . .'

'But nothing. Say nothing. Just do it. Think of the reward at the end. You'll be rich and you'll be free and there are not many orphan brats in the Two Kingdoms you can say that about.'

Can it be that simple to follow the path to freedom, I wonder? In the end, it doesn't matter as I like my neck the way it is, and Imi's too. So I nod.

'Good,' the Quiet Gentleman says. 'One more thing: Thutmose won't tell me who the contact is, but I reckon it's one of the old priesthood, maybe even the former high priest – Panhese. When the old religion went, he lost all his power. He'll still be angry.'

I nod dumbly. The only questions I have he can't answer. How did I get myself into this situation? And how do I get out of it?

29. In which I leave my sister

I'm woken up before sunrise.

The cook's assistant bustles me out of the workshop towards the kitchen courtyard where she pours water over my head and soaps me all over. Then she smears some revolting oil in my hair, hands me a stone and tells me to scrape the worst of the dust off my feet. When I'm clean, she hands me a new loincloth, a new tunic and a pair of new sandals.

It's awful saying goodbye to Imi. She knows I'm going away and is trying to be brave, but when I say I'm doing it so we can go home she bursts into tears, proper little girl's tears, because she's not home and wants to be. So I promise her that things will be all right and she just has to wait, and the huge cooks snorts and the assistant dabs her eyes and then it's time to go.

We're escorted to the palace by a squad of six soldiers. They are bare-chested, muscular and carry spears and shields. Two lead the way, Thutmose's slaves lift up his litter, then I follow with four more guards behind me.

We pass under the bridge where I saw the royal family for the first time and stop by the first great palace gateway on the left. Its high towers claw the sun-baked sky. Close up, the red banners look tatty and dusty.

Our squad leader, suddenly very official, barks out an order and slowly the huge wooden gates creak open. I notice that the wood is thin and cracking, and the gates scrape across the ground as they open. Thutmose gets out of his litter and we're pushed through the doors. The soldiers who escorted us stay outside as the doors are dragged shut behind us. We're in.

To our right is a sandy square, lined with giant statues of the king. Every face the same: huge eyes, hollow cheeks, full lips, and they are staring at each other over the remains of a banquet that's been abandoned. Rows of tables are strewn with dried-up food, palms leaves lie browning on the ground by upturned benches and loose awnings hang limply in the heat. Crows and vultures are pecking over the remains. It's so quiet I can hear their wings flap as they fight for scraps.

To our left is the front of the main building, glaring white and as high as a cliff. A new squad of soldiers is waiting for us. We are marched out of the bright light and down a wide corridor into the darkness.

The place smells of dust. Some rooms are full of rubble. In others, rickety wooden scaffolding covers the walls. Through the lattice of poles I catch glimpses of fantastic painted scenes: of the river or fields, marshland or forest. The colours are so bright they make the world outside seem dry and dull.

'My designs, my work,' Thutmose barks at me, then, 'By the gods, what's happening here?'

He jabs his stick towards a workman who is mixing colours. 'Those are not my colours and that is not my design! Who are you? Just a common slave! This is what happens when I'm not on hand to supervise.'

He raps at the wobbly scaffolding and high above us a paint-spattered man, who is working on a complicated frieze of leaves and flowers, calls out in alarm. Thutmose is still complaining when we are ushered into a small, square room where a man with a face like a hawk is examining a plan spread out on a table. Light spears down from a row of high square windows. When he sees us, he holds up a hand to halt us in our tracks and lifts a weight from one side of the plan, letting it roll up with a snap.

Thutmose gets down on to his hands and knees and bangs his forehead on the floor.

'Oh, Mahu, Great One, forgive my humble intrusion and accept my thanks for allowing me into your sight, blessed with the brightness of the Aten, but I understood that I would be seeing the mighty Panhese, high priest to the king.'

I see a smile creep across Mahu's face. 'You may have to wait a while. As head of security I like to see what and who is entering the palace.'

'I am sorry, One Who Basks in the Glory of the King. But Panhese . . .'

'Is . . . otherwise occupied.'

'Then later?'

'Are you deliberately trying to hurt my feelings?' says Mahu. 'It was I who invited you to the palace on hearing the news of your glorious recent achievement and all you can talk about is the High Priest.'

Mahu sweeps his gaze over the box in my hands. 'And is this the wonder? Is this the crowning glory of your skills? Could it be the gift you promised the Most Beautiful Queen, the Image of Approaching Perfection, when was it? Two years ago? May I see it?'

'Oh, Great One, it would take a lifetime to do justice to her beauty, but it would be . . . improper to have such beauty exposed to the eyes of others. Until of course she has seen it.'

Mahu looks at Thutmose, eyes narrowed. 'Rise,' he orders.

Thutmose pushes himself to his feet with a hiss of breath and cracking joints.

'Hold out your hand,' Mahu says.

Thutmose extends his arm. His hand trembles then starts to shake harder. He mutters something that sounds like a curse and lowers it.

'I see my spies were right,' Mahu says with a smooth smile. 'Are you quite sure you want your queen to be the first to see what those feeble hands have done?'

'But Panhese . . .' Thutmose protests feebly.

'I say this in the spirit of friendship, but it is my strongest recommendation that you forget all about Panhese and perhaps think more about me. It is the queen who will be inspecting your gift, not Panhese, and you, old man, know what she's like when she's angry. Still, as you will. Wait here.'

He leaves the room. Thutmose collapses on to a nearby bench. He is sweating and giving off a terrible bitter smell.

'This is dreadful, boy. Not what I anticipated. We must rescue the situation, yes, indeed. We'll see the queen and then we must make sure we see Panhese.'

'Why?' My question is ignored as Thutmose carries on talking.

'And if we have the great honour to be brought before the queen, do not look up. Do you understand? Let me do all the talking. I understand her. She is worried. She is insecure. She must be flattered, but she is no fool – she didn't always live a pampered life in a palace. She can read a false heart like a scribe reads a scroll.'

'Yes, master.'

'Don't pretend you have the slightest idea what I'm talking about! If we are tested, if anyone asks us to make changes to the sculpture, we do not do anything here, you understand? We work in the workshops, not in the palace. Is that clear?'

'Yes, master.'

'Compose yourself. I can hear people coming. This will be the greatest day of your life. You will be taken into the queen's presence. You will be breathing the same air she breathes and living in her light.'

His tone has changed and he sounds like a lovestruck idiot. I can keep my wits about me better than he can!

But then an official with a shaved head and wearing a white skirt appears in the doorway and beckons to us. I pick up the box and follow Thutmose's tottering steps further into the palace.

30. In which a boy discovers he can look at a queen

Off a great hall a long corridor of red-painted pillars recedes into the distance. At the end of the corridor is a chamber, in the chamber is a throne and on the throne is the queen.

Still as a statue, she is lit by a single shaft of sunlight that falls through a high window. She is wearing the high crown topped by a serpent. A wide necklace of gold chains and bright blue gems falls over her breasts.

Thutmose and I are stopped from walking any further by a vast man with flesh as white as milk and as soft as butter who steps out from behind a pillar.

'Down,' he says, and Thutmose and I press our foreheads to the floor. I count fifty footsteps as his fat feet slap the flagstones. I risk a look and see him talking in the queen's ear. Fifty paces back.

'Approach Perfection,' he orders in a hoarse, powerful voice and walks back.

Thutmose begins to wiggle forward and I do the same, pushing the box in front of me. When we are less than halfway, Thutmose starts to babble about radiance and majesty in a quavering voice. His mouth is so close to the flagstones that it's hard even for me to hear what he's saying, but he gets his timing right. At the precise moment we reach the toe of the fat man, he gets to the point: 'This radiant image of the Radiant One is ready to be graced with the brightness and beauty of the radiant eye. Will she accept this humble gift from her humblest slave?'

A silence. A very long silence. I break it by pushing the box further forward with my fingertips. It scrapes across the floor with a sound that puts my teeth on edge.

'Thank you, master craftsman. If the art of your hand matches that of your tongue, then we are indeed in for a delightful surprise,' the queen says. Her voice is low and slightly sharpened by something like sarcasm. 'However, I am sure you did not mean me or the princess to open the box.'

'Your Radiance?' A pause. I look sideways. Thutmose is craning forward and turning his head this way and that. He tries again: 'Your Radiance, I did not want to presume to display my humblest of tributes to the Radiance's beauty until the Radiance . . .' He runs out of steam and snaps: 'Boy, open the box!'

I hardly hear him. A single word is still screaming in my ear: princess. THE PRINCESS! The one person in the world I can't risk seeing me. She must be behind the queen somewhere, in the darkness at the side of the chamber. My stomach is as hollow as a cave. I barely register that Thutmose is prodding me with his staff.

'Boy!'

Nothing for it. I squirm up and on to my knees with my

head bowed and start to fiddle with the catches. The box has been made so that the sides fold down when the lid is lifted and the sculpture is left standing on the base. If I can work it right, then hold the head so it's in front of mine, perhaps the princess won't see me. It's a complicated manoeuvre, but I manage it and stand up.

'Ah,' is all the queen says. Just: 'Ah.'

'Turn it, boy, turn it!' Thutmose hisses.

I turn it to the left and I turn it to the right, not all the way though. I think it looks best sort of half turned. From straight on and from the sides, the head is perfect, like a goddess. Half turned, you see the person I glimpsed in the temple.

There's a rustling as the queen stands. I am staring hard at the floor. No one has ever got to know a piece of floor as well as I know that one.

Now she's standing in front of me. Her feet are as soft as hands, I notice, and long. Her toenails are painted. Her sandal straps are sewn with little jewels. Her dress, folded into a thousand pleats, is tight around her ankles then swells over her hips and belly. You can sense the body underneath; I can smell the heavy perfume she is wearing.

'Hmm,' the queen says.

She is walking round the head now, looking at it from all sides. A pause.

'Is Your Radiance . . . pleased?' Thutmose asks.

'She is pleased,' is all the queen says. 'This . . . conforms.'

I have no idea what she means. She walks away so I can no longer see her. I wish someone would ask for a table because my arms are beginning to shake. If I lower the head now, the princess will see me.

'Mother, may I have a look?'

There it is – the voice I dread.

'Of course, my dear. I would like to know what you think.' The queen's voice softens as she talks to the princess. Honeyed but a little tense.

I feel my face flushing red; I half close my eyes and try to control the awful trembling in my arms. I hardly hear the light tread of the princess. She is barefoot. Her feet are slender and soft like her mother's and the thought comes out of nowhere that she couldn't run across the desert or even walk down the street barefoot without cutting her feet.

She too stops in front of the head, then examines it from each side. The closer she comes, the tighter I close my eyes. As if that's going to help.

'Master craftsman, this looks just like the queen,' she says.

'It barely does her justice. The perfection, the . . .'

'Blah blah, radiance, blah blah, perfection, blah blah, beauty. No, I mean it looks like her. How can this be?'

I can feel Thutmose's confusion. 'It is the new style of art, Your Highness. The new decree is that likenesses should be likenesses and not . . . er . . . the divine image.

And Your Highness should understand that her mother's beauty is famed throughout the Two Kingdoms, throughout the worlds beyond, even to the heavens themselves. She is the Crown of Creation, the Aten's gift to the world and . . .'

'So did the god tell you that when she frowns, two tiny lines appear between her eyes?' the princess asks. 'That's not very . . . kind of the god, considering the effort she makes to try and hide them. From common little people like you, I mean.'

It's like the room has taken in a sharp breath. Thutmose's breathing suddenly becomes a bit wheezier. I can almost hear the thump of his old heart. Sweat breaks out on my forehead. It's not just my arms that are shaking now. I feel as if I'm going to faint and I'm sure Thutmose does too. He gasps: 'My . . . er, I feel . . .'

'Someone bring a stool for the old man, and a table so this slave can put the head down,' the princess snaps.

Footsteps – servants appear from nowhere. A table is plonked down in front of me. I unscrew my eyes, put the head on it and descend to the floor again. Have I got away with it?

But it's Thutmose who has the princess's attention.

'Do you feel better now?' she asks. 'Are you ready to answer? Look up – I can't hear what you're saying when you're being so tremendously and irritatingly humble.'

Thutmose tries his best. 'My Lady does not understand.

Such beauty as the queen's is heaven-sent. All I had to do was dream of the most beautiful face I could imagine and then render it humbly in my materials. As it is, it falls far short of the queen herself.'

'But I thought the new decree demanded that it should look like her? I repeat: it does, but just a little bit too much. It's almost as if you got really close to her and stared and stared and stared . . . Is that possible?'

Thutmose makes a sound like a bleat. There's nothing else he can do. But the princess is relentless.

'And if you didn't, maybe you sent someone else to spy on her? And if you can't talk perhaps your slave can help. Slave, do you know how the craftsman made such a good likeness of the queen? You see, it is one thing to make a likeness that looks like a god, but this . . .'

'He did it!' Thutmose's voice is cracked with fear. His finger is pointing straight at me. 'He did the work. I was always going to tell you. I don't know how he managed to create such a likeness – it must be magic, sorcery. The old gods talk to him. They guide his fingers. Oh, the shame! The blasphemy! I had no hand in it. We brought it only to show Your Majesty so she could be aware of the danger she is in from . . .'

A sudden handclap stops his babble. High above, a clatter of wings seems to echo the sound.

'Enough,' the queen says. 'Meritaten has had her fun. Thutmose, is this true?'

Before Thutmose can invent another lie, the princess interrupts. 'Don't ask *him*. Make the slave answer.'

I press my head into the floor so hard that either skull or floor is going to crack.

'Stand, slave.'

I get to my feet. Somehow.

'Open your eyes.'

The light that slants into the room from the high window turns the dust in the air golden. I force myself to look at the queen, who is beautiful, and the princess, who is beautiful as well. I place my hands on the model of the queen's head. 'Thutmose started it, I finished it,' I say. 'I beg for mercy. I did not know what I was doing.'

'So the master craftsman thinks so little of his queen that he uses slaves to make their image?' the queen says.

'It's not like that,' I say. 'He was stuck. He didn't know what to do. I can . . . make things in the new way. So they look like people.'

The queen turns to me slowly. 'And you made me?'

I glance at the princess who seems delighted by the question. She recognises me – there can be no doubt about it now – and she's just waiting for me to say the wrong thing.

'Not you. I made the model. That's all it is. It's just a model.'

'And do . . . the gods . . . talk to you?'

I swallow. Nothing can save me so I may as well tell the truth.

'In the past, the old gods talked to me. They were hiding in the mud and my hands talked to them and they talked to my hands. Now, here, it's different.'

But as I am talking, everyone's attention is shifting away. The guards behind the queen have lowered their heads, and now the queen has, and the princess too. Thutmose has thrown himself flat again, but like an idiot, I turn to see what's going on behind me.

A god has entered, and then I realise that I'm only thinking that because he is dressed like the old statues in the deserted temples. This is not a god. This is the king.

He is wearing a royal crown, the royal dress and is holding a sceptre. His necklace of gold and stones is so broad it covers his chest. He is very tall. His face is long, his eyes are dark and calm and his lips are full. But everything about him is slightly wrong and his copper skin radiates weirdness like a fire gives off heat. Under that towering crown, his head is slightly too small. The hand holding the sceptre is too thin and the arm cradling it is too long.

Ignoring everyone, the king walks over to the queen's head and looks at it, long and hard. Silence stretches out like catgut tightening.

Mahu is in the first rank of noblemen behind the king and is the first to talk.

'My Lord, what would you have us do?'

The king is looking at the model of the queen's head so intently that I think his gaze is going to burn through the paint, burn off the plaster, get down to the stony lump of skull underneath.

The queen has returned to her throne. Her skin is taut across her face and her expression is fixed, just like the model's. But just as that head is made of layers, so is her expression. The outer layer is calm, but under that there's anger. And under that there's fear.

'My Lord . . .' Mahu says again. His voice tails off as the king looks away from the head.

'The slave lives,' he says. 'The old gods may hide in the mud, but the Aten finds them. They cannot hide there forever. But the slave made one mistake. He said he made this. But he did not. The Aten made this. He sees all. He saw the queen and he showed the boy. I am pleased.'

He nods to the queen and then his gaze sweeps across me, pauses and moves on. He walks out, courtiers following like an unruly tail, gossiping already. Some break away to walk over to the head and stare at it; some even touch it, and when they do, I see the queen flinch as if they had touched her own face.

31. In which my new life begins

The people trickle out of the audience chamber. A servant carries the sculpture. Two guards frogmarch Thutmose away, but leave me behind. I am too frightened to move and don't know who to follow, so I wait.

A white dove feather floats down from on high, flares in a sunbeam, drops, drops, drops and settles on the queen's throne. For the first time I notice the paintings on the walls of the throne room.

Wonderful scenes. Palm trees and birds, hippos and crocodiles, fish and fishermen. The colours are brighter than real life so each scene stands out: there's a tree with red and turquoise feathered birds in it but there, half hidden by the branches, a grinning cat is stalking them. A fisherman casts his net from a boat while the fish swim in the other direction. A buffalo sinks his head towards the water to drink, unaware of the crocodile beneath the surface.

'Stop gawking and follow me!'

It's the big pale man who was with the queen. From his neck to his waist is a slope of wobbling fat. Waist down to feet is a long white apron. His face is bland and round. He wears an odd cap on his head and has very dark eyes.

'Come!' His mouth is an ugly slot and his skin so

smooth it looks as if it has never seen a razor. He leads me out of a door at the back of the chamber. For all his size, he waddles quickly, bare feet slapping on smooth stone. He doesn't look back as he talks.

'My name is Potipher. I am the queen's chamberlain. That is a general storeroom . . . Assistant grain master's office . . . Grain master's office . . . Hall of scribes . . . Office of ink mixer . . . Antechamber to eastern throne room . . . Small corridor . . . Slave's corridor . . . What is my name?'

'Potipher?'

'And what am I?

'A chamber . . . a chamberman?'

'Hah! Not a chamberman nor a chambermaid. I am the chamberlain. I manage the queen's household.'

All I see are rooms and doorways and corridors. Dark rooms and light rooms. Big rooms and small rooms. I trot after Potipher, trying to remember what he says, but knowing it's going in one ear and out the other.

'Where are we going? What am I doing?'

He ignores me.

The corridor is lit by oil lamps with small flames that emit trails of black smoke. The air is warm and damp. You could stir it, like soup. Then it gets lighter and we walk up some steps past a window and I realise that we are on the bridge over the Royal Road where I first saw the princess. I glance out of the Window of Appearances and see the road below me and the window ledge I climbed on to. It is only then that it finally sinks in: I am in the palace. Me. Mud boy.

But I have no time to think as I trot after Potipher, across empty courtyards and echoing halls, down more corridors until –

'Your room.'

He points to a small, square room. In it is a sleeping mat and a jug. Nothing else apart from woven rushes on the floor and a window too high to climb out of. 'Stay and food will be brought. In, in, go.' He shoos me in as if I'm a chicken.

'What am I doing here? What's going to happen?' I say.

'You're part of the palace now, part of the staff,' he tells me. 'This is your life. We'll wash you and train you and shave you here properly (he rubs his head) and here, if you know what I mean,' he says, pointing to below his waist. 'Maybe that will be later. If you are obedient and clever you may grow to become like me.'

He stands very still so I can observe him, this towering mound of obedience and cleverness. 'Once you are chosen, you are chosen. You are in the palace now and you can never leave. What is your name?'

'People call me boy,' I say.

'Descriptive,' he says. 'Adequate. Temporary.'

He pushes me back into the cupboard and locks the door.

32. In which the queen gives me a name

Never leave? This isn't part of the plan and I know what he meant by shaving me down below. Men like Potipher who serve important women have their manhood cut off so they are not tempted. I don't want that. I don't want to be here at all. This is nothing like the way the Quiet Gentleman said things would be. I crawl on to the bed and curl up. I get to thinking about a cat in a well I saw last summer.

You could see it, swimming round and round, daylight pooling in its eyes. The women lowered a basket, but it wouldn't get in and, in the end, a child had to be lowered down on a rope to fish it out. The cat fought like a devil all the way up and scratched the child badly, but he had to hang on because you can't have a dead cat stinking out your well.

So why am I thinking of the cat? Here's why.

1. When you're scared, you act stupidly.
2. You might not recognise help even when it's dangled in front of you.
3. No one rescued the cat for the cat's sake.

If I'm going to get out of here, I'm going to have to be clever and not expect anyone to help me.

I must have dozed off because I wake up and find Potipher gazing down at me.

'What were you dreaming of?' he asks.

'Pussies in the well,' I say.

'Try again.'

'How best to serve the queen.'

I think he smiles. There's a sort of twitch of the mouth. 'Good.'

He leads me back along the corridor. He's like a duck – his top half doesn't move, his legs can't be seen but he really shifts. Sweat beads on his forehead and smooth pale arms.

'Your instructions: don't talk unless she asks you a question. Don't answer a question unless she asks you to. Keep your answers short unless she wants them long. Don't look at her. When you enter the room, fall on your face. Don't get up unless she talks to you. If you have to leave her presence, walk backwards, looking at the floor. Don't turn your back on her ever.'

I'm out of breath. Sweat is now running off the fat man, darkening his apron at the waist.

'One other thing,' he says. 'You are safe for the moment, but be very careful. You're in the palace now. The most dangerous place in the Two Kingdoms.'

Before I am taken to the queen, my head is shaved properly by the oldest woman I have ever seen. Her back is as round as a beetle's, her mouth looks as if it's being sucked past her gums and her skin is like worn linen.

She pushes me down on to a low stool and gets going with the scissors. They make a dry, metallic sound and when they touch my scalp my skin crawls. After that she oils my head and starts to shave it. I rub my hand over my scalp. It reminds me of my father's chin after he's been to the barber. My head feels lighter. I feel different – more alert.

She leaves me to wash myself, thank the heavens, and I put on a new loincloth and a simple tunic of white linen. Potipher looks at me and nods.

'You are ready,' he says. I am anything but.

The queen is in her courtyard. Everything is gilded by the afternoon sun. Set around the courtyard are deep, shaded awnings and in the middle is a raised pool of dark water. At one end is a wooden throne covered in beaten gold and the queen is pacing up and down in front of it. Trailing behind her, a little bit sulkily, is a woman plucking a little harp. As she passes the ranks of attendants, they bow their heads like wheat bending in the wind.

'And if that's not enough,' the queen is saying, 'that snake Mahu was with the king. Ever since he arrested Panhese for treason he's been altogether too big for his boots. I bet it's him that's trying to push me into the north palace. We must watch him.'

As she passes, I throw myself on to the floor dramatically so she will notice. She doesn't, but the attendants turn and stare at me, as one. Some giggle. They are all women; they are all young; this is a nightmare.

'What is it?' she snaps, then sees us. 'Oh, Potipher, it's just you. Approach, approach! Bring the . . . boy.'

I scramble up and follow Potipher and throw myself to the ground when he stops, just for good measure.

'You may rise, small boy who did not bow to the king,' the queen says.

I swear there's amusement in her voice, but I am too busy being humble to take a peek. I stand, but keep my eyes fixed on the floor.

'Now,' the queen says, 'you can tell me who put you up to this. Who told you to pretend that you made my image, that you sculpted my head? And why?'

I sneak a sideways look at Potipher. He jerks his head.

'Now?' I whisper too loudly because everyone hears. All the girls closest to me laugh.

'Yes.'

I open my mouth, but it's too dry to say a word.

'Potipher, what did you tell him to make him so scared?'

'I told him nothing, Most High One. Your beauty has struck him dumb.'

'Then I have grown more beautiful than the last time we met because he talked to me then. Boy. Look up.'

In case it's a trick, I look up with my eyes closed.

'Boy. Forget what this wobbling eunuch or anyone else in the palace has told you to do. Open your eyes and tell me who put you up to this. Now!'

Her voice snaps out like a whip. All laughter stops.

'Put me up . . . No one. I mean . . . I just . . . I don't understand.'

'Then understand this: I have never seen you, but somehow you have been able to study me so closely that, when I look at your work, it is like looking at myself. That is impossible. Whose work is this? What palace spy? How could anyone think I would fall for this trick?'

'But it's not a trick,' I manage to say. 'I mean . . .'

'You dare contradict the queen?' Potipher's voice rises in a hoarse shriek.

'No, that is . . . I just . . .'

'By no you mean yes?' the queen hisses, drawing out the S like a snake.

'I can just do it,' I stammer. 'I can just see someone with my eyes and then it's like my hands see them as well. It's not just people. I used to do animals – cows, crocodiles, horses . . .'

My voice trails off as I hear shocked, disbelieving laughter, suddenly cut off.

'You would compare the queen to a . . .' Potipher begins. His pale skin has taken on an even sicklier, milkier colour. I look round and see the same reaction everywhere. The attendants are mostly looking down, although some are staring at me with their mouths open.

'I didn't mean it like that,' I say, but my voice is as faint as the skitter of a beetle across the floor. 'I just meant I can make things. But I never did someone like you before. You were my first, Your Beautifulness.'

Then comes a sound I didn't expect. The queen laughs. It is a warm sound, unexpected and very real.

'The last person who said anything like that to me was the king on our wedding night,' she says. 'Now, boy, if you were any cleverer, you might have been in trouble, but I think you may be the only honest creature in the Two Kingdoms.' She turns to her handmaidens. 'Ladies, beware: do not ask him questions in case he decides to tell the truth. Anyone who can honestly compare a queen to a cow is dangerous indeed. Does he have a name?'

Potipher looks taken aback. 'Not that I know of, Highness.'

The queen climbs to her throne and, with a gesture, orders one of the attendants to bring me a stool.

'Boy,' she says, 'talk.'

And once I start, I can't stop. I tell her about my life from the moment my father pulled me out of the water to the moment I was brought before her, though I stick to the Quiet Gentleman's story about visiting an aunt down south. I don't tell her about seeing her in the temple of course – I'm nervous enough of the princess without involving her in my story and, when I have finished, all she says is, 'You have the look of an outlander about you. Perhaps you floated here from heaven in your straw boat to be found by a queen. It pleases me to think so. People call you boy, you say. Others call you mud boy. I shall call you Boy Who Did Not Bow To The King. A strange name, but you are a strange creature.'

Then she calls out: 'Potipher, I know the custom is to cut the boys and men who work in my palace, but leave him whole for the time being. He's too young to be trouble and I don't want him sickening. Then give him mud or clay or gypsum or some other form of muck and we shall see what he can do.'

33. In which I receive a proposition

Now the queen has spoken to me, I'm suddenly the centre of attention. Her attendants make a fuss of me. They want to know what I can do and one of them gets hold of some clay and they all want to watch me make something.

I look around at them, all beautiful, all expectant, and some instinct tells me not to try to make an image of one of them. If I do a good likeness, the others will be jealous. If I do a bad one, I'll have made an enemy.

So I do Potipher instead, cruelly, and then they all want me to make funny heads, which is fine and not dangerous and I can't fall foul of anyone's jealousy. The younger children of the royal family, Mekataten, Ankesenpaten, Setepenre and Tutenaten, are brought in for their daily visit. Three princesses, very quiet, and the young prince. He's the baby of the family and spoiled by his sisters, who take turns to put him on their knees. When the queen orders me to make models of them out of clay, Tutenaten ruins each one and no one cares. The queen doesn't seem very interested in them and I overhear one of the handmaidens whisper that all she wants is Meritaten to visit. I pray she stays away.

And so the first day passes.

On the second day, the queen fires questions at me. She has never been north and she has never seen the pyramids, which she calls by their proper name: the Houses of Ascension. She shakes her head disbelievingly when I say that they are taller than the highest tower of her palace, wider and deeper than its greatest courtyard and shine white in the sunshine like crocodile teeth. I tell her about the City of the Dead at the feet of the great pyramids and the empty temples where wild dogs now live, but she gets a lost look in her eyes and interrupts me.

'Do you think I'm beautiful?' she asks.

'Yes,' I say, honestly shocked.

'There are great kings and queens buried in the Houses of Ascension,' she says. 'Does anyone remember their beauty?'

I swallow. The tombs in the Pyramids were robbed

centuries ago; surely she must know that? But her question gets me thinking about my job here.

'When I am dead, at least people will know my beauty and that is because of you, Boy Who Did Not Bow To The King,' she says in a tragic voice.

She orders me to hold up the model of her head and stares at it hungrily. 'This will never grow old,' she says. 'This will stay young forever even when I am in my tomb.'

She grips my wrist when she says this. I feel the dampness of her hands. My skin is wet with the sweat of the queen and I know I try to get her to talk more about the tomb, just in case I can pick up clues about it, but there is something awful and sad going on behind her eyes that makes my throat clench.

Time passes and life should be good. Although I'm locked up at night, I have my own room. The food is like the food of the gods: meats and breads and fruit and sweet things. The attendants peck at it and find fault wherever they can. I eat as much as I can.

No one hits me. No one hurts me. No one expects me to do anything except make little clay models and, after the first day's excitement, there's less and less of that.

I try to learn the attendants' names: there's Kiya, Neferupta, Te, Seshemetka and Satiah. There's one that comes from a land far, far away whose name sounds like a horse drinking. I get a bit lost after that.

On my third day, the handmaiden called Satiah beckons me to sit with her by the pool. I like her because she never strokes or pets me just because the queen happens to be passing. If she's kind, it's because she wants to be. I notice her because she doesn't want to be noticed.

It's the middle of the day when the heat is more like a deafening sound that echoes off the walls. The air shimmers. All the other attendants are lying in the shade, taking turns to fan each other. Satiah couldn't send a clearer signal that she wants to get away from them. She asks me where I'm from, and when I tell her about my life outside the palace, she looks sad and distant.

'I have never been outside,' she says. Her fingers are trailing in the water and big, lazy fish are nibbling them. 'The first thing I remember is working in the kitchens as a little child. When I got a bit older they trained me to dance for men in the palace. When the queen saw me doing cartwheels on my own, she brought me here. That was four years ago and I've never seen the outside world. I tried to get up on the walls once, but I was caught and Potipher beat me. I just wanted to see the Great River and the palm trees . . .'

'What's the queen like?' I ask.

'The queen is like the queen,' she answers.

'But why am I here? I thought I'd be put to work, making things for her, but she doesn't seem to care. Why doesn't she let me go?'

'She'll never let you go. This place is a trap. You can only go deeper and deeper in.'

'But what I am supposed to do?'

Satiah shakes her head. 'Nothing. She just wants to keep you away from the king. She thought you were an agent of his, you and that old craftsman who looks like an evil crow. They don't get on, you know.'

'The king and queen?'

'There are no secrets in the palace. The king doesn't talk to her any more. A few years ago he spent as much time in her court as he could. Now he stays on the other side of the bridge, surrounded by his courtiers and that Mahu, the chief of police. He wants to move the queen to a new palace on the edge of the city so he can marry again and install a new wife here. The queen wants to fight back, but what can she do? When she saw the model of her head, it scared her.'

'But why would the model of her head make her worried?' I ask. 'I don't understand.'

'Idiot! She told you.' Satiah hits the water with the palm of her hand. Fish scatter. 'It means you must have spied on her and she doesn't see how you could do that without the king's help. If you are the king's spy, she cannot kill you without making him angry. And if she can't kill you, then she must keep you close.'

'But none of that's true,' I say. 'How can I be the king's spy? I never met him. I just came here . . .'

And I stop again. How can I tell her my real reason for being here?

Just then a lazy voice drawls from the shady side of the square. 'Satiah, what are you doing over there with your boyfriend? Trying your luck with a real man?'

There's the sound of a pillow hitting someone and a muffled *ooff*. More giggles. Satiah stands up crossly.

'See what you've made happen,' she snaps. 'Now the others will tease me and for nothing.' She storms off.

The girl with the lazy voice is called Sekmis. She's big and beautiful and looks as soft as a cushion. Without doing much she seems to get all the other girls scuttling around her.

But what I have noticed is that she's always watching and never really relaxes. So when the queen is having one of her lie-downs, or one of the other girls is painting her eyes or polishing her nails, Sekmis has a group around her. Every now and again the group's eyes will swivel to one of the other girls, fix on her and then there will be a sudden peal of laughter. And when that happens, even the queen wants to know what's going on and will dismiss her helpers and let Sekmis bend down and whisper in her ear.

The girl from the north whose name sounds like a horse drinking runs over to me, making a great play of fanning herself as she comes. She has high, slanting eyes and skin the colour of ivory that she has to keep out of the sun.

'Sekmis wants you,' she says with a jerk of her head. It

all sounds a bit like I'm being summoned, but I'm tired of being pushed around. I look down at the water and pretend to be interested in a fish. She turns so they can't see her. 'Please,' she begs. 'It's just a little thing . . . if you don't come, Sekmis will punish me. Please.'

The two girls who are excluded are the obvious outsiders. Foreigner or dancing girl, it doesn't matter.

The flagstones are so hot they burn my bare feet. It's a relief to get into the shade. Sekmis is lying on her side and looks at me from under her heavy eyelids. She makes a little pout and pats the cushion by her.

'Now then,' she says. 'It must be better to be out of that horrid sun?'

I look at her cautiously. 'I thought he was the god,' I say.

'Oh, no one takes that seriously here,' Sekmis says with a little smile. 'Do we?'

There's some careless laughter to show how unseriously it's taken.

'We're the queen's attendants. We leave all that to the king,' Kiya says. 'We were just wondering what Satiah wanted with you. Did you know that she's a spy?'

'For who?'

'The king of course. You don't think he wants to know everything the queen is doing?'

Sekmis shushes her. 'We don't know that, darling, do we? It's just a little worry we sometimes have. You have to watch some of the people here. Be careful what you say, and if Satiah does start asking you questions, just remember you don't have to say anything. You didn't give anything away, did you?'

'No,' I say. 'But the way she was talking, it was like she thought I was the king's spy.'

Sekmis snorts. 'She thinks she's so clever. But what on earth made her suspicious?'

I decided to tell the truth. 'She wanted to know how I made the queen's head so lifelike,' I say.

Sekmis smiles. 'Oh, that. I wouldn't worry. Everyone needs to have their secrets, don't they?'

She's fixed me with a knowing smile. It's an 'I know something about you' smile. In spite of the heat, something deep inside me feels very cold.

The moment passes. She brushes a hand across her forehead. 'Ah well, it's time I got up for my bath. You can help me, can't you?'

'Have a bath?' I stammer.

'He's growing bold,' she says to a wave of giggles. 'No, silly. I meant you can help me get up.'

Blushing so hotly that my face feels like it's melting, I hold out a hand, which she takes. She stands, bends over me and seems to be about to give me a kiss. Instead, her mouth just brushes my ear. 'Be ready tonight,' she says. 'The old woman will come for you.'

And then the attendants disappear through the doorway to their quarters. And me? I don't know what to think.

34. In which Potipher delivers unwelcome news

I can't relax for the rest of the day – there's so much to think about.

It bothers me that Satiah wants me to talk; it bothers me more that Sekmis wants to talk to me. Everyone needs to have their secrets. Which of mine does she know? That I'm a murderer? A tomb robber's accomplice?

Half of me wants the night to fall now, while the other half wants the day to stretch out into forever. For the evening meal, slaves lay out a huge feast, but I feel too sick to touch a morsel. When the meal is over, the girls drift off to do whatever it is they get up to in the evening and Potipher escorts me back to my room. He locks me in, so I don't get up to mischief, he says, but just before he closes the door he puts a hand under my chin and lifts my head.

'Are you sickening?'

Because I don't want to tell him that I'm sick with nerves, I say that I might be.

'Because if you are, I'll have to keep you locked up all day. The queen's terrified of plague.'

'Oh,' I say, 'I'm not so bad. Not really. Just feeling a bit homesick. That's it.'

'Home,' he says blankly. 'The sooner you stop thinking of that, the better.'

I lie down and hug myself. I can hear servants through the door and high window: sweeping, washing dishes or just going about their business. They make me feel less alone. But then the sounds drop away and the silence presses in on me like a coating of soft dust. I have to escape. But how?

I roll over on to my back, my head centred on my wooden pillow, and imagine the hard brightness of the moon, stars moving across the sky, the fleeting scratch of a shooting star . . . Imi used to say that every shooting star was a god coming down to earth and my father would mutter, but only when she couldn't hear, that it was another god dead.

Perhaps I sleep. There's a scrabbling at the door. Fear is like a splash of cold water and I sit up as the bolt is pulled, the latch lifts and the door opens a crack.

Light spills through the gap. I get up as if I've been pulled on a string and follow it. The light comes from a little lamp and it's already a few paces in front of me. I recognise the hunched back of the old woman who shaved my head, but she doesn't turn round to see if I'm following. She just shuffles on and I begin to feel as if I'm in a dream. The air is still, warm and the darkness presses like velvet. The light falls on closed doors, moves past a larger corridor that I think I recognise, then climbs up some stairs . . .

I get close to the old woman. She smells of charcoal, woodsmoke, cinnamon.

'Where are we going?' I whisper. Whispering seems like the right thing to do.

'You'll find out soon enough.'

'But we're leaving the queen's palace.'

'Count yourself lucky. Not many do that.'

We're crossing the bridge between the palaces. The moon is high above the Royal Road and the palace buildings on either side glare blue-white. And then we're down the other side into the king's palace.

'Where now?'

She places a bent finger across her thin lips. I can see each finger segment is tattooed with a little X, very black in the moonlight.

'Guards,' she breathes. She points to the end of a long corridor where lamplight shows. 'I know ways.'

And with that she pinches the wick of the lamp and plunges through a doorway into the darkness. I can tell it's a great hall by the way our footsteps sound, hers light and limping, mine a steady, nervous shuffle. Then she's taken hold of my hand, forced my head down and we're in a narrow space that smells of plaster. It is pitch-black and the corridor is so narrow my shoulders are brushing the sides.

On we go and on. Then we're out into a normal corridor, moonlight filling slitted windows, so I can see long rows of doorways and statues. A public corridor then, but where?

At the end a great door is open a crack. I peer through and try to make out what's inside.

'At the back of this room there are six doors. Take the second from the left and walk on to the last door on the right.'

I stare into the darkness, think I can see a line of doors on the other side of a pillared hall.

'Am I to go on my own? How am I going to get back?'

No answer. I look for the old woman, but she's gone.

35. In which I am led astray

I panic. I think I hear faint footsteps somewhere in the darkness and start towards the sound, but suppose it isn't her? Fear of being alone struggles with fear of being caught, which wins.

I slip into the hall. It is so huge I can't make myself walk across the middle of the floor. I skulk around the sides, count off the doors and slip through the second from the left. A corridor with light coming from the last door on the right.

I tiptoe down, my heart racing. I can smell the candles from halfway down the corridor. I knock softly. No answer. I look in. The heat from the candles is overwhelming – it's like sticking my head into an oven. I see a bed, carved at the head and foot and looking like a fabulous boat. Cushions are scattered all over the floor. The walls are painted with dark trees, crowded with brightly coloured birds. On the far wall, someone has built up a stack of furniture under the window.

I stand stock-still, utterly confused, sweating in the heat.

Suddenly a head appears at the top of the window, upside down and with hair hanging in a dark waterfall. Then I hear the one voice I dread, and her laugh.

'There you are, baldy. You're late. Come up on to the roof. Hurry – or I'll have you killed!'

The princess is waiting for me on the roof, smiling. 'You took your time. We're going to have fun. Follow.'

And she's off, running across a flat roof that seems to be as wide as the Great River. Beyond that is another higher roof and we scramble up.

It's like another world. There is nothing but the roof beneath my feet and the huge sky above me. In spite of everything, I feel free and as light as a bird as I hurry after the princess. There's another step up with a row of square windows set into it.

She puts her finger to her lips, then gestures for me to peer in. Below is a long corridor. Immediately beneath us, a long way down, two guards are talking in low voices. The princess picks a lump of plaster off the wall and flicks it through the window. It lands on the ground with a little chink. The guards don't notice. She takes a bigger lump and aims more carefully.

It hits a shield. There's a cry. We both jerk back and

flatten ourselves against the wall, me wanting to scream in terror, she with her hand pressed to her mouth, smothering her laughter. We hear a cry, a clash of metal, silence, then voices. We peer over. One guard is looking up the corridor, the other is looking down. They are crouched. Alert.

The princess is clambering up on to the next level and darting across it.

'What did you do that for?' I ask when I catch up with her. 'We could have got caught.'

'But you don't get caught, do you? No one bothers to look up. They're so stupid.'

'And if they did?'

She smiles. 'But they never do.' And she's off again.

As far as I can see, we're right in the centre of the palace. In one direction is the Great River, the moon laying a white bridge across its surface. To the north, I can see the white walls of the Great Temple and beyond that what looks like another palace that I haven't noticed before. Then there's the desert all around, hemmed in by a jagged line of mountains.

'Look! My father's building me a palace there.' The princess points to the south. 'And that's my temple. He has the big one and I have the small one. It's good, isn't it?'

I nod.

'That's not very enthusiastic,' she says.

I say what's in my heart. 'I don't know what I'm doing

here. You saw me in the sun temple, and then you saw me with Thutmose. And now this.'

She frowns. 'Oh, you think I'm favouring you, but you're not worthy,' she says. 'I see.' She pauses, biting her lower lip with her little white teeth. 'Look at it this way. If you saw me pick up a little kitten, say, and play with it, would you think: why is she doing that?'

I shake my head.

'What would you think?'

'That the princess thought the kitten was pretty.'

'And if you saw me reach up to a fig tree and pluck a fig, bite into it, then spit, throw it away and order that the fig tree be cut down and burned, would you think: why is she doing that?'

'I would think that the fig was bitter or spoiled.'

'It would not have to be bitter. If it was not perfect, that would be reason enough for me to have it destroyed.'

'But that's wrong,' I say. 'Another fig might have been just right. It's not the tree's fault you picked the bad fig.'

'And you don't understand a thing,' she said. 'I would order that tree destroyed for the same reason that I played with the kitten. Because I wanted to. Now do you understand?'

I spread my hands. 'You have me here because you want it?'

'Yes. And when I want it, I will have you struck down, which is what I wanted to do when you were presenting

165

that sculpture to my mother. All that talking – so boring. It made me sick. Anyway, it's better doing this than hanging around the royal court, waiting for nothing to happen. Come. I want you to see something.'

We head north. A small roof is raised above the others and windows are set into the wall. She gets on to her belly and crawls to one of them. It is shuttered, but a hole has been picked in it. She looks in for a while then rolls away.

'You look,' she says.

I put my eye to the hole and peer in.

It takes a while for my eye to adjust as the moonlight is bright and the room I am looking into is dark. The air is thick with incense. I see statues, things gleaming with the soft lustre of gold. Below me is a bed and I'm looking straight down at it.

Lying on it is a man. He is on his back and very still, dressed only in a white loincloth. His head is shaved and his eyes are painted with dark lines and they are staring straight up at me. I jerk my head back, heart thumping.

The princess starts to laugh. 'Not scared, are you?'

'He was looking right at me!'

'Was he? Look again.'

I have to force myself, but I manage it. We're invisible, I tell myself. I can look for as long as I like, even if he has got his eyes open, but the longer I look, the odder it seems. His eyes don't move and, as far as I can see, they don't blink. Is he a statue? No, I can hear him breathing, or think I can. He turns his head slightly and the eyes move with the head.

'They've been painted on,' I say. The princess walks away and sits on a low parapet. We're facing the desert behind the city and in the distance, in the moonlight, I can just see a dark line of mountains.

'He likes to keep watch. I think deep down he's scared.' For the first time, the princess seems just a tiny bit thoughtful.

'Who?'

'My father of course.'

My head snaps round to stare at her. 'That's the king?'

'Didn't I say?'

'No!'

'Am I very bad?'

'Yes.'

'You wouldn't think that if you knew what I had to put up with.'

'What you have to put up with?' I blurt out. 'I've been kidnapped. My sister's a prisoner. I was almost turned into a eunuch and still might be as far as I know. That's what I've got to put up with. How can you say you have to put up with anything?'

'You've been free,' she says simply, 'haven't you? When I caught you in my father's temple – all right, the sun's temple – you were there because you were free, even if it was stupid and blasphemous. I'm never free. There's always someone watching me, telling me what to do.'

'But you don't have to do it,' I say. 'And you don't do what your mother wants. You never come to see her. She always looks out for you, you know?'

A little smile of satisfaction lifts the corners of the princess's beautiful lips. 'Hah,' she says. 'I'm glad you told me that. It serves her right. The king and queen fight over me, but they fight about everything. My mother gives me stuff, my father gives me more. Gold. Silver. I once asked for an elephant and he gave me ten. It gets boring after a while, but my mother's too strict . . . No wonder my father wants her to move to the north palace. She's no fun and neither are you for making me think about this.'

'How can I make you do anything, princess?' I say.

She gives me a look and that seems to be the end of our adventure. We trail back to her room and she sends me back into the pillared hall.

'You know,' she says, 'I'm going to see you again. You're more interesting than most people but I don't know if it's because you're almost clever or very stupid.'

The old woman is waiting at the end of the corridor. She leads me back to my lonely room and locks me in. I hardly seem to have closed my eyes before Potipher is prodding me with his toe.

36. In which the queen favours me

The attendants are tense and snappy as they sit around the pool this morning and look as sour as week-old milk. To keep herself entertained, the queen has told them to play catch with a wooden ball. The girls have to toss it across the water to each other and if it falls in, the queen decides whose fault it was and they have to pay a forfeit. Sekmis gets splashed when the ball falls short and then throws it short herself to splash Satiah.

'Enough,' the queen says. 'I don't know what's got into everyone today. I just want people to have fun, to enjoy themselves, and what do I find? You fight like starving cats over a scrap of goose fat.'

Sekmis is quicker than Satiah. 'Forgive our selfishness,' she says. 'We were not thinking of Your Royal Highness, only of our own little disagreements.'

'I'm tired of it. Tired, do you hear? Potipher, to me!'

There's a whispered conversation, and then I feel Potipher displace air behind me.

'We are going to the north palace,' he says in my ear, bending so close I can feel his breath. 'To punish her handmaidens for bickering, the queen wants you to bear the royal fan as we walk. It is an honour far greater than you deserve.'

And that is how I come to be walking by the queen's open litter, waving a huge fan of ostrich feathers above her head while the crowds are held back behind a row of spear-wielding guards.

It's a long walk down the Royal Road. The buildings fall away, the crowds fall away, quite suddenly as we pass the Great Temple. Now we have the desert to our right, the river to our left and in the distance, just showing through the heat haze and dust, the north palace.

'What do you think?' the queen says suddenly.

I walk a few paces before I realise that she must be talking to me. The handmaidens are following in a long train, two to a litter. No fans for them because the queen is displeased.

'It's, er . . .' I squint through the dust. 'It's big?'

'It is adequate. Should it please me?'

I have been long enough in the palace to sense a trap, but not long enough to know quite how to avoid it. I can stall for time though.

'What does Her Radiant Brightness think?'

'That whatever its qualities, for me it will either be too small or too large, too low or too tall, too dim or too bright,' she says.

'Then I agree. The palace is too small, too large, too dim and too bright,' I say. 'Such a shame.'

'And the decorations?' she asks.

'Much too colourful and far too dim,' I say confidently.

'We are inspecting them today. That is exactly what I told your old friend Thutmose a year ago. I hope he has had time to reconsider,' she says. Pauses. 'You will enjoy seeing him again. Perhaps you can tell him what I want?'

'Is that an order?' I ask.

I dare to look at her face. It has lost its look of pinched tension. For a second she almost looks amused and interested. A fly lands on her nose and she waves it away.

'Keep fanning me,' she snaps. 'Never forget your duties.'

Thutmose is waiting for us at the gate to the palace. The gate is bounded by two high towers and opens on to an empty courtyard, white walls glaring in the sun.

'What do you think of it so far?' the queen asks me. 'Hold the fan so it shades my face.'

'I think it is very bright, Your Highness.'

As Thutmose raises his head from the ground, a bit of dirt stuck to his forehead, he gives me a look that a cat might give a bird, out of reach on a branch.

'As do I,' the queen answers. 'Master craftsman! The courtyard is too bright.'

And so it goes on; she asks me if the throne room could be bigger. I answer, truthfully, that it could. Could this bedroom be smaller? Yes, indeed. Thutmose has a scribe following, scratching the queen's instructions on to a slate. The scribe fills up the good side and is forced to start on the rough.

Thutmose manages to walk beside me while we pass from a minor throne room to the palace offices.

'What are you playing at?' he hisses.

'If the queen does move in here, I'll have to go with her and then I'll be locked away forever,' I hiss back. 'No chance of our plan ever working.'

'What are you two whispering about?' the queen calls.

'He was saying that your joy is his only goal,' I call back. 'As it is mine.'

Thutmose frowns, but then he's scuttling off to the queen who is standing in front of a brightly painted relief. This one shows the king and queen seated on twin thrones. The sun is above them, sending rays down towards the family. Every ray is covered with gold and ends in a tiny hand that is blessing the royal couple.

'Your Highness, surely this is to your pleasure?' Thutmose asks. He is practically wringing his hands.

The queen has stopped dead in front of it. The king and queen are made to look alike, with strange, elongated skulls and oddly swollen bellies. It is hideous and I am about to say so when the queen speaks.

'I like this,' she says.

Thutmose relaxes. 'Now I know what delights Her Highness, I can ensure that every detail of her new residence is to her liking.'

'You misunderstand me,' she says. 'I like it and I want it removed from this palace and installed in my present

172

rooms. I want it in a place where the king will see it and my . . . and where the Princess Meritaten will see it.'

And then I spot it: the tiny figure of the princess, standing between the thrones, holding up her hands to the rays of the sun. She barely comes halfway up the queen's calves and the sun's rays do not meet her.

On the way out, Thutmose pulls me back. 'Have you made contact yet?' he whispers.

'With who? There's no sign of Panhese. No one knows where he is.'

'He's dead,' Thutmose answers. 'Executed for treason. But there is another.'

'What? But that's . . .'

'A detail. Keep to the task in hand. You're in too deep to back out now.'

'But I never get to see anyone,' I say.

'You must try harder,' Thutmose answers. 'Your sister is missing you. Such a shame if she died of a broken heart.'

'Boy Who Did Not Bow, approach!' the queen snaps.

I feel sick with anxiety and guilt about Imi, but I have to obey the queen's summons.

'You have pleased me today, boy,' she says. 'You have shown loyalty and quick wits. Tomorrow we ride through the city: the king, the queen, their children and a few chosen attendants. I will choose you. It is an honour.'

I bow and manage to say thank you.

'I would expect more gratitude than that,' the queen

says. 'You may well be elevated from court monkey to court member. People have killed for less in the Two Kingdoms.'

'Thank you, Your Highness. I'm sorry, Your Highness,' I answer. 'It was seeing Thutmose. He reminded me of my sister – I came to the City of the Sun's Horizon with her and she misses me. I wish there was something I could do.'

'A sister? You have a sister? Of course there is something you can do. Once you are elevated, all you have to do is ask for her.' She smiles. 'But you are not quite there yet.'

37. In which I do not ride in a chariot

It is a hot, still morning. We have assembled in the courtyard of the king's palace, watching a host of chariots trying to arrange themselves into a line. The queen stands on her own, her attendants behind her. Then her children, including Meritaten. Then half a dozen officials. They look at me as if I'm dirt and shuffle me out of the way so they are standing in front of me like a wall.

At last the chariots get into some sort of order. The horses' hooves echo on the walls of the courtyard as they bring the chariots round, and as the king's glittering silver chariot reaches the front of the line, he appears in the entrance to the palace. He walks slowly, swaying slightly, the sun making his broad gold necklace gleam. At his chariot, he stops. The queen steps forward and bows to him. She waits, as if expecting him to mount the chariot, but instead he turns his head slowly to where the royal children are standing and nods.

Meritaten walks towards the chariot and a gasp goes up from the court officials, quickly stifled as we hear the queen say: 'My Lord?' in a strangled voice.

'The princess rides with me,' the king replies. 'Today we shall ride the full extent of the city, from boundary to boundary. This matter concerns her.'

'And why does it concern her?' the queen asks.

'It concerns her because it is of concern to her,' the king replies. 'When she takes her place next to me on the throne, she must know the land of which she is queen.'

His expression does not change. It is odd, this massive calm that radiates from his long, strange body, and it breaks the queen. I can see her shoulders slump as the king climbs into his chariot, Meritaten following.

Then the queen straightens her back.

'If His Royal Highness rides with his daughter, I shall ride with the Boy Who Did Not Bow To The King,' she snaps.

While she is saying this, she is ushering her children away from the next chariot. 'You, into the next one. Boy! Come with me! I shall not ride alone.'

I step out from behind the courtiers, but as I do, a figure appears from nowhere and blocks my way. It is Mahu.

'Stay there,' he orders.

'But the queen . . .'

'You will do as I say. I have been to the city and to the workshops of Thutmose,' he says under his breath. 'And I have seen your sister. Do you want to see her dead? Do. Not. Move.'

The queen says: 'Boy?' but it is not an order. Shock, disappointment, hurt . . . I hear all those feelings in that little word.

Mahu turns to face her. 'The boy will not join you unless you pick him up and sling him over your shoulder,' he says. 'Now, My Lady, the king is waiting for you. It is time to join him and his bride-to-be.'

I watch her turn and climb into the chariot with the king and the princess, her husband and her daughter, her husband and his wife-to-be. I feel sick with myself, and sick at the way Mahu has managed the queen's public humiliation.

I look for him, but he has melted away. Now Potipher is surging towards me, his fat rippling. He looks furious because I have let down the queen and played my part in her downfall.

Basically, I am in Deep Trouble.

38. In which I pay for my mistake

Potipher keeps me locked in my room. Slaves bring me food, but they don't talk or even look at me. By the time evening falls I'm feeling hard done by, and when Potipher comes to check on me, I try to explain what happened.

'There was nothing I could do,' I say. 'I wanted to go to the queen, but Mahu stopped me.'

'None of that matters.'

'But I've got family in the city! Mahu said he would hurt them if I moved.'

Potipher regards me impassively. 'You did what Mahu told you to do, not what her highness wanted. From her point of view, you are the hand that no longer holds; the mouth that no longer sounds. You are withered, you are empty, a rattling gourd, a flap of skin. You are dead to her. She has amputated you.'

When I hear the lock turn in the door much later I think it's Potipher come to kill me, but it's not. It's the old woman. The princess wants me. I am an empty gourd, a flap of skin carried wherever these lethal palace winds want to take me.

This time the princess has brought food up to the roof: bread, fruit, pastries, mutton . . . It's been laid out like a feast.

'I made the cooks give it to me,' she says. 'Slaves carried it up. I'll have them killed if they tell. Come on. We're going to be the king and queen.'

I stare at her. 'What?'

'I'm the queen and you're the king.'

'But I'm not the king,' I protest. 'And the king wants to . . .'

'You're always boasting of being able to make things; make yourself into the king. Come on, it can't be hard. He hardly talks. He just stares.'

My first attempt at making myself the king makes her burst out laughing. 'You look like a pregnant cow,' she says. 'Honestly, his face isn't that bad.'

So I open my eyes a little bit less and tighten my jaw.

'Better,' she says. 'And what would My Lord have me serve him from this sumptuous feast?'

I take her advice and don't talk. I simply incline my head every now and again, and look calm and regal while she talks about the food and the guests that aren't there and all the plans she has for changing the palace once her mother has been moved . . .

'You're moving her?' I blurt out.

'Quiet! Oh, you've ruined it. Completely ruined it. Of course I am, when I'm queen.'

'But how can you do it? Your mother . . .'

'You're so stupid. You've ruined everything. Don't talk about it. Off you go. Go, GO!'

But the old woman comes for me again the next night. I find the princess has forgiven me and is in a different mood. We lie on our backs on the highest roof of the palace and she makes me tell her all about the old gods in the sky and how you can see their outlines in the stars. I watch her and she watches the stars. I want to hold her.

The next night and she's in a different mood again: she's wild; her eyes are dancing and she's looking everywhere but at me. She says she wants to do something exciting so we head north to an area of lower roofs of differing heights that make a black-and-white pattern of squares: moonlight and moonshadow.

Just before we get to it, we stop. 'Well? Are you brave enough?' she asks.

'For what?' I ask.

'For anything I say. Are you brave enough for that? Last week I took a beaker from one of the courtyards and put it in the one next door.'

'And someone got into trouble?'

'Perhaps. Do you think that's wrong?' She smiles and her eyes slide sideways, showing their whites. I shrug.

'What's wrong with you this evening?'

'Nothing, apart from being locked in my room all day and worrying that your mother might have me killed at any moment. And my sister. I can't stop thinking about my sister all on her own at the workshops.'

'What a lot of things to be worried about,' the princess

says. 'First, you won't be killed because my mother can't think of a worse punishment for anyone than not being allowed to see her. Second, my father doesn't think you should be killed. Third, I don't see why you should worry about being locked in when there's nothing else for you to do. Fourth, if you're worried, it means you're not thinking about me so I disapprove.'

'I just want to know my sister's all right.'

'Hmm. Would you do anything to find out?'

'Yes.'

'All right. You steal something for me then and I'll help you.' And she runs off.

The princess must know every corner of the palace roof. We follow a twisting path on the walls between courtyards and clamber over a few small rooftops. These buildings are still attached to the palace, but they are not grand halls: storerooms, I'm guessing, and offices.

The princess stops and points down into an empty, doorless courtyard.

'There,' she says. 'There's no way in or out of that courtyard, but the builders left a ladder on the roof. We could lower it together and climb down. If you come here in the evening, you can hear people talking and there are scribes and people making tablets.'

'What are the tablets for?' I ask.

She gives a little snort. 'The king has to know everything and everything has to be noted on a tablet: how many barrels of oil were sent from the north, how many tons of wheat, how much gold was captured when he raided the Nubians, what sort of tribute was sent by the Assyrians. It's all noted and written on clay tablets. All the food for the Aten, all the materials for the palace, all the plaster for the king's tomb, everything.'

My heart starts to thump. 'So whose office is it?'

'The king's architect, I suppose,' she says casually.

'And plans?' I ask, hoping my voice isn't shaking. 'Will there be plans?'

'Probably.'

What follows is one of those moments where my mouth says something before my head can stop it. 'Let's do it then.'

The princess's eyes open wide with delight and there's something in the way she looks at me with her dark eyes, the way the smile hovers on her lips. I return the smile and take a step towards her. I want to hold her face in my hands. I want to feel the softness of her skin, I want to . . .

Her eyes narrow. 'Slave,' she says, 'you're acting strangely. I didn't bring you here to stare at me. I brought you here to prove you are worthy of my help.'

'I'm sorry,' I say.

'Good. To make your test even better, I'm going to send you down alone and you have to come back with something precious or I shall scream until the whole palace is woken up, and then they'll make you scream. Go and fetch the ladder.'

181

The ladder is spindly, light as an old bone. I climb down, trying to ignore the splinters under my hands and feet. Down in the courtyard it seems much darker and the air is warm and dusty. I see a doorway and move cautiously across to it.

The dark wraps round me and the smell of papyrus seeps from the room. I know it from the scribes that used to visit my parents' inn. Normally I like the smell. It's green and fresh, but in here it's so strong it suffocates. As my eyes grow accustomed to the dark, a thousand eyes stare at me from the walls.

My heart pounds, but it's not eyes of course – it's just the round ends of scrolls stacked on shelves from floor to ceiling. I take one out at random, then move to the doorway so I can look at it by moonlight.

Writing, neat and densely packed. I have never seen so many words. They murmur to me, but they say nothing I can understand because I can't read. What was I thinking? That the first scroll I put my hands on would be a map with a picture of a tomb and a great big cross to mark the spot?

I pull out two more. The same: line after line of dense writing. I put them back and choose another two, but a sound from outside makes me look up.

At first I think my eyes are playing tricks because I can't see the ladder. Then the truth sinks in: the ladder is gone and I am trapped.

39. In which the trap closes

In the courtyard, I call as loudly as I dare: *'Princess, princess!'* but I know she has abandoned me.

In panic and rage, I throw myself at the wall, trying to claw my way up it. I scrape my face, tear my fingernails and almost twist my ankle as I land badly. Then I collapse, chest heaving, bitter spit gathering under my tongue.

How could I have trusted her? What part of me didn't see that she's a monster? I know the answer: the part that wanted to impress her. The part that wanted to believe that, in spite of all the evidence, up there on the rooftops, away from the palace, a slave whose name no one knows could be on a level with a princess, even for one night.

Idiot! Now what? I must find the door out of the office and try to get back through the palace, but I'm halfway across the floor when I hear voices. There's a table pushed up against a wall and I just manage to scuttle under it as the door opens.

Lamplight on the floor. Two pairs of legs.

'You heard what?' It's Mahu's voice and he sounds furious.

'Noises, master. Rustling.'

'And you woke me for a rat or a cat?'

'It sounded bigger, master.'

'Lift the lamp higher so I can see . . .'

'Master! The scrolls have been disturbed! Every night I leave them perfectly arranged. There, two have been misplaced. This is a grain record and it's been put in the oil section. See?'

Mahu's voice is measured. 'You are sure?'

'Without a doubt. But how did they get in, master? Ever since we've been working on the new project, I sleep in the corridor outside, as you recommended. No one could have left by the door without stepping over me.'

'What about the special project?' Mahu says. 'Has that been disturbed?'

From my vantage point, I watch the scribe walk to the far corner of the room. More rustling. 'No. It looks fine.'

'Check it,' Mahu snaps.

'This is the main tomb,' the scribe says. 'This should be the inventory . . . receipts to craftsmen . . . plan outline, plan details. Yes, yes. All here.'

He rolls the scroll up, then puts it back into its place on the shelf. Mahu checks it, and in his desire to make it secure, he pushes it deep into the rack so I can mark exactly where it is.

'In all my years, master, I never heard of such a thing. What times we live in. I must get some water.'

'Very well, very well.'

Their voices change as they walk out of the office and into the courtyard. My heart starts to hammer. I mustn't think, I must just act. I move quickly, but it seems as if I'm moving slowly. I'm being quiet, but my breath is roaring like a hurricane. I know what I've got to do, but I can barely think. So in a sort of rushing dream I stand, take the scroll Mahu put back and, as quietly as I can, I tiptoe out of the door.

The scribe's mattress lies across the threshold. I step over it and scan the corridor. My instinct tells me that the queen's palace is to the right and that's the way I run.

It's as if I'm weightless and my feet have wings. At the end of the corridor I turn left, then right down a wider passage. No one's about, no one's following me. I pass the odd servant sleeping in a doorway or curled up in a corner, but I run past as softly as I can, trying to ignore my growing tiredness and heaving breath. I stop. Does that corridor lead to the bridge? I take it and am in luck, but there's a guard at the entrance. I flatten myself against the wall, trying to pant quietly, and luck is on my side again. He is going off duty and his replacement is walking towards him from another direction, sword clanking impatiently against his small shield.

I wait until they meet and exchange a few jokey words, and then dart across, as quiet as a mouse. I glance out of the window as I cross the bridge. The sky is getting light. People will be rising soon and I cannot afford to be caught, especially with the stolen scroll.

I'm almost dead on my feet by the time I reach my room

and I'm too tired to look at the scroll. I stuff it into the gap between my mattress and the wall, then collapse. Even as my mind races with the events of the night, I drop into a deep, dark sleep.

40. In which I do not learn a lesson

It feels like only seconds later that someone starts to kick me. I open my eyes to see Potipher's face glaring down at me.

'Get up, boy,' he says in his odd, hoarse voice.

'W-What?'

'Why is your door unlocked?'

From deep sleep to sickened shock in the thinnest slice of time. I can see the top of the scroll sticking up from the side of the mattress where I stuffed it hurriedly the night before. I pretend to stretch and move to cover it, looking up at Potipher's quivering belly.

'I don't know what you're talking about,' I yawn.

'I lock you in every night. This morning I find your door open. Either I have made a mistake or someone has been in here.'

I shrug. 'I slept heavily. I don't know.'

Potipher places his palm on my forehead. It is dry and surprisingly cool.

'You feel hot. You had better stay in here today. The plague is sweeping up from the south, and however careful we are in the palace, it is hard to keep it out.'

'But I haven't been anywhere to catch it,' I say. 'You know that.'

'Plague strikes without warning. In the old days they said it was when Sekmet stretched out her arm. Now they say it is when the Aten is angry and sends an infected ray towards the earth.'

In the distance I hear the clash of metal and shouted orders.

'What's that?' I ask.

'The palace is in uproar,' he says. 'Thieves broke in last night. They got in over the wall – tomb robbers most likely – and Mahu's searching the palace to see if they're hiding.'

I widen my eyes and sit up straight. 'Do you think that a thief might have looked in here last night?'

Potipher shrugs. 'I'll report it. I hate to think what'll happen to any thief Mahu finds.'

He leaves, locking the door behind him. I get up and check the door really is locked, then I take the scroll from its hiding place, panic fluttering inside me. Where can I hide it? The first place they'll look is under the mattress and there isn't anywhere else. Could I burn it? Eat it? Perhaps I'd better look at it first. I put my ear to the door – no one's outside – and unroll the papyrus.

A lot of straight lines with writing all around. I stare

and stare at it, but it means nothing. I turn it round and round. Holding it one way makes it look (a bit) like a snake; holding it another way makes it look (a bit) like a man with a sickle. The writing looks like writing. A load of birds and people and eyes and squiggles. It might be a plan. It might even be a plan to the king's tomb. So this is what I'm suppose to smuggle out with the queen's head, but how do I do that? The head is with the queen and the queen won't see me. I'm as stuck as I always was.

And then I suddenly understand something. I see how I can escape from the palace and get back to Imi. Brilliantly, wonderfully, it's the princess who has shown me the way. All I have to do is get back on to the rooftops with her.

And then make my move.

41. In which I make a sacrifice

But the waiting is awful.

I panic when the door is unlocked later in the day, thinking it's the guards, but it's only someone bringing me food. I doze, staring up at the high window. I think of the princess and wear myself out trying to catch the thoughts chasing through my mind. My mood switches from fury to hurt and back again. I don't know which is worse: the thought that she wanted me to get caught so she would be rid of me, or the thought that she was simply playing a cruel game.

At last the high window darkens, turns black and the stars scratch their slow course across the sky. When the door is opened by the old woman, it's a shock. I'm very, very nervous.

Stealthy old time has been stealing slices from the moon. It's lower in the sky and the night is darker. I can see the princess's teeth when she smiles and the glint of starlight in her eyes, but she doesn't smile often and her voice is low and serious.

'I thought I might not see you again,' she says. 'So I'm glad you're here.'

A little twist of joy twitches in my heart.

'I thought perhaps you might have been too scared to see me again.'

'Why?'

'In case I told you to go and get something else.' She breathes in, then out. 'Would you?'

'Of course,' I say, my heart thumping in my ears. 'In fact, why don't I steal something better for you than a stupid old scroll?'

This is my brilliant plan: I've made a rough sling from a sheet and wrapped the scroll in it. I can feel it under my tunic. So all I have to do is offer to steal something else for a dare. The princess, according to my plan, will look delighted and we'll set off across the rooftops. But instead of stopping where she says, I will just keep running, running, running to the edge of the palace and then to freedom . . .

But she's talking: 'You think that's just a stupid old scroll? That stupid old scroll only happens to show the exact location of the king's tomb and its layout, and Mahu's only gone and arrested half the architect's staff. You seem to have got lucky, slave boy. But what's that you're carrying?'

She grabs me. Feels me. 'It's the scroll, isn't it? You brought it with you. What were you thinking of?'

'Nothing.'

'Don't lie, slave boy. Don't lie, slave. You brought it for me.'

'Yes.'

'It was a gift? Or did you want to get me into trouble?' She's like a bird, pecking here, pecking there, pecking for the truth.

'No.'

'Then what? You were going to run away!' Her eyes widen. Her mouth opens. 'That's the truth, isn't it? That's what you were planning.'

'I just need . . .'

'You were going to leave me. You must hate me.'

'You left me in the courtyard! I nearly got caught!'

'I'm the princess. I was testing you. Anyway, there's something you don't know.'

'What?' I feel freedom slip away.

'The last person who tried to steal those plans was my father's head priest. He wanted to know where my father was going to be buried so he could steal all his grave goods. And do you know what Mahu did to him? He strangled him with a little rope and then pegged him out in the desert for the sun to look at. Except, I think wild dogs ate him up. So Mahu is very loyal and Panhese was not. Mahu is alive and Panhese is dead. And Panhese was stupid too. Do you know why?'

I am about to answer when out of the corner of my eye I see movement. I turn my head and it's gone. It's like that at night: the darkness only allows you to glimpse things.

'Shh!' I say. 'I heard something.'

'An owl. What is the matter with you?'

'Look!'

Now I know the movement is not in my imagination. There's something on the edge of the wide roof to the left and to the right. Now I see the glint of moonlight on metal and I know what is happening: soldiers are moving fast to cut us off. I grab the princess's arm and point. Her eyes widen.

'I can't be caught with you!' she says. 'It'll be the end. My father will hear of it and it'll be me that's banished to the north palace.'

'But –' I start to talk, but she interrupts.

'What can I do? I could lose everything. You must help me. You must!'

I see the moon in her eyes and the stars in her tears.

'Please,' she repeats. 'Please.'

I do it like a coward. I throw away my future like a coward, lying to myself that if I do this she will see me in a whole new light, while deep down I know that it is just something she'd expect from any of her slaves.

'Lie flat,' I say. 'The roof is white and so is your dress. They won't see you. I'll draw them off that way so you can run back to your room.'

So I dash across the wide, flat roof, keeping low for the first twenty paces or so, then straightening up so I can be seen.

The soldiers shout; the plan works; I am caught on the roof with the scroll. I have thrown away my one chance of getting away and of saving Imi. I am definitely dead.

42. In which I learn that death leads a dog's life

Mahu has me. His office is a bare, square room, quite large, with hauntingly dirty walls. There is a table in the middle of it on which I am lying.

His men tied my wrists, slammed me face down on the table and beat me on my back and the soles of my feet. I cannot describe the pain. It's as if they are beating the me-ness out of me. When they hauled me upright, my feet burned and ached and the pain moved up my legs, up my back, my neck and into my head.

I have been standing in Mahu's office for a very long time. An hour? Two hours? Half a day? A lifetime?

The scroll is now the only thing on the table. A guard stands between me and the door and threatens me with a baton if I move too much. Sometimes Mahu comes in and stares at me, then goes out again, then comes back as if he's waiting to see a change in me, something to tell him that I'm ready to talk.

When he finally speaks, it's not how I imagined at all.

'Well, time for my meal and then a snooze, I think. Oh, be sure to wake me if he decides to talk.'

'I've got nothing to say,' I protest.

But Mahu is talking to the guard. 'They all crack in the end, even hardened criminals like him,' he says.

'I mean, I don't know anything.'

'They all pretend not to know anything,' he says to the room in general. 'They should just save themselves the trouble and talk straight away.'

I might as well not exist. I am just the bits of me that talk – a throat and a mouth and not much else.

Mahu leaves, then pokes his head round the door and this time he looks at me. 'In case you'd forgotten, I'm interested in that.' He points at the scroll. 'That and how you got on to the palace roof.'

And goes again.

Time passes. My feet hurt, my legs hurt, my back hurts, my head hurts and now I'm thirsty. It's a feeling that takes over my entire body, pushing out the pain. I just think of all the times I was near water and didn't drink. I can't believe I didn't drink whenever I had the chance. My need to drink is a desire I never knew I could feel. It's in my mouth and throat . . .

Mahu looks in again. 'Probably getting thirsty by now, I wouldn't wonder. I drank a lot of water with my meal. Cool, crystal-clear water. Water that trickled down my throat. He'll not get a drink until he talks,' he says to the guard.

In the corner of the room with dirty walls, darkness has gathered and thickened. It is now taking on the shape of a big, black, snouty dog. He is very doggy, even though he is standing on his back legs. He is staring at me and panting. His teeth are yellow and his tongue is as black as mud.

'Woof, woof, woof,' Anubis, the god of the graveyard, says. 'Why were you on the woof?'

He walks away. His legs bend backwards at the knee. When he walks, he bobs and sways. He lifts an awkward back leg, pees against the doorpost and is gone.

I fall. Water is thrown on my face and because my mouth is open some of it goes in. I suck the floor.

'I have something to show you,' Mahu says.

His guard picks me up. I am cracking like a mud brick in the sun and I weigh as much as dust.

We go out of the palace into the warm, pressing night and an empty back street. And another. Mahu knows where the empty streets are. We are following Anubis, who sometimes looks over his shoulder at me and rolls his long, mottled dog lips back into a toothy grin. His smell is a brown trail in the air.

We are passing out of the town to a square hut that stands on its own, the clean desert behind it, builders' rubble in front.

'Does he want a bit more water?' Mahu says. 'Open up.'

I open my mouth and he squirts a mouthful of warm, leathery water into it from a goatskin. It spills from my mouth and balls in the dust to make mud.

'Want you to keep your wits about you,' Mahu says.

I smell death and herbs in the still air. Death, herbs, spices and incense. I swallow. Is this it? Is this where I die?

'I want to show you something,' Mahu says. 'I want to show you what I am up against and why it is so important you talk to me.'

A tall man and a short man are waiting outside a small house. It looks to me as if they've been beaten up: the small man has a black eye; the tall man has a split lip. They are dirty and their clothes are torn.

'Do you know this boy?' Mahu asks.

The tall one stoops and looks at me closely. 'Don't think so. Should I?'

Anubis walks past them and merges with the dark behind the door.

'You were caught performing death rituals in the holy city without a licence,' Mahu says. 'You are in trouble. The only chance of lessening your sentence is if you tell me the truth.'

They look at each other, eyes wide. They don't want to tell the truth but they want to avoid another beating. The small man looks at me; the tall one looks at him. The small one licks his lips.

'So talk,' Mahu says. 'Talk to the boy. Don't leave anything out.'

The man begins to talk. His voice is a flat monotone. 'We lay the body out. We prepare it for . . .'

'Details,' Maku interrupts. 'He's young. He loves the gory stuff.'

The man nods. 'If the body is fresh, we open a vein on his leg and we hang him up so the blood drains out. His head is full of grey stuff. We push a long spoon up his nose. There's a thin bone inside and we break through that and then we break up the grey stuff so it runs out of his nose. We call it giving him a cold.'

He wheezes, his shoulders rising and falling, and I realise with a slight shock that he is laughing at his own joke. 'Then we cut the body open with a knife. We start just below the ribcage and work down. We take out the lungs and we take out the liver. We take out the pancreas

196

and the kidneys and we put them all in jars. We take out the stomach and we take out the guts. We leave his heart in because it must be weighed in the afterlife. If he's done wrong, his heart will be heavy and he will never be allowed to go to paradise. Then we take the natron . . .'

'The boy doesn't know what natron is,' Mahu says.

'It's white powder from the earth. It comes from the north. It dries the body out. We fill the jars with natron and we fill the body with natron and we leave it. I can show you . . .'

He steps back humbly and ushers us through the dark doorway. The air is musty, sweet with rot, spiced with perfume. Along one wall are rough wooden boxes, all empty apart from one which is full of gritty white powder, like salt. The man brushes away at it and a pale, leathery face is revealed.

'Almost ready,' he says to his companion.

'And do you have a lot of work? Are you kept busy?' Mahu asks in a measured voice. 'I need to know the extent of your corruption so I can gauge the offence to the king.'

The man gives a hopeless shrug. 'Not really, but there's no other work here and this was my craft before I came to the city. I need to eat.'

'And Panhese, the king's high priest? What did he want?' Mahu asks smoothly. 'Did you go to him or did he come to you?'

'How did you . . .?' the smaller of the two men begins before the taller one jabs him viciously with his elbow.

'Shut it!' he says desperately.

'Too late,' Mahu answers. 'Too late,' he repeats, almost sadly. 'But it was always obvious. Now you need to answer me in order to spare yourselves much pain.'

'He came to us,' the smaller man says. 'An important man like that? It was a dream come true. He asked a lot of questions, I'll give him that. How much oil would we need, how much natron; if we were short, how long would it take to get new stock – money upfront, not that we saw a penny of that. It would have been a lovely mummification. Proper quality.'

'Interesting,' Mahu says. 'And it never occurred to you to ask why the high priest, the *king's* high priest, would want to use an unlicensed outfit like yours? No? How odd. I wonder what he could have been thinking of.'

'I don't know. We were just honoured.'

'And now the high priest is dead. Executed for treachery.' Mahu turns to go. Turns back. 'Oh, by the way, from what you say, I gather Panhese expected to be using your services soon. He didn't give a date, did he?'

'Within the month,' the small man says.

Mahu nods and turns away again. He says to his guards: 'Kill them quietly. No fuss. Leave their bodies inside then burn the place down. All that oil will burn well. Boy, we'll talk back at the palace. I expect you'll want to explain what's going on.'

One of the guards picks me up and another leads us back through the sleeping alleyways, into Mahu's quarters at the back of the palace.

'What is the glory of the Two Kingdoms?' Mahu asks me when we are back in the big, dirty room. He waves the guards away and lets me sit on the floor. 'Our towering pyramids? Our magnificent temples? The Great River? Our terrifying armies?'

'All of them,' I answer, wondering what on earth this has got to do with anything.

'None of them. The clerks are the glory of the Two Kingdoms. They weigh and measure everything and they write it down. Every ounce of grain. Every drop of oil. Every inch of cloth. Every side of meat. They measure, they record and they manage. A bad harvest and the price of grain will go up. The price of grain goes up and the price of bread goes up. The price of bread goes up and the people become unhappy, so we release grain from the royal granaries or I employ more secret policemen to take out the troublemakers. So while the clerks measure grain, I measure threat. I measure danger.'

'To the king?'

'To the kingdom. Always to the kingdom. Which is where you come in.'

'Me? A threat to the kingdom?' I exclaim, jumping to my feet.

'Yes, you,' Mahu says. 'A boy who appears out of nowhere. He can walk through walls. He can fly on to rooftops. His fingers talk to mud. I dig a little deeper. He is from a slum in the north. He has arrived on a boat. A man is murdered on the boat. He finds his way to some workshops. Those workshops belong to Thutmose, the royal craftsman, and no time at all, this boy from the back of beyond, the very end of nowhere, is installed in the royal palace currying favour with the queen herself. Do you recognise this boy?'

I nod, though I admit it all seems rather amazing. Mahu's eyes have not left my face.

'You see, I am a humble man and when I don't understand something I'm not too proud to ask simple questions,' he says. 'Who brought this boy to the city? Who helped him walk through walls and fly on to rooftops? Or perhaps it doesn't matter. Perhaps it is not the boy I should be thinking about, but the people behind the boy.'

This time I shake my head, thinking of the trail that will lead back to Imi.

'Very well. You were brought into the palace to steal the plans for the king's tomb.' He gestures to the table where the scroll is still lying. 'I know that, so don't deny it. But you never asked what use a tomb without grave goods is to tomb robbers.'

'I never thought,' I say. I feel stupid. I think the princess was about to make the same point just before the guards appeared.

'And you never thought that the best way to ensure a tomb is full of grave goods is to put a body in that tomb?'

I shake my head.

'But you agree.'

'Yes, but there is no body,' I say. My mind feels stubborn and blockish.

'But there would have been,' Mahu says patiently and flatly. 'Why do you think Panhese the traitor went to an unlicensed mummifier's workshop? He is a priest so he wants to do things properly. He is a traitor so he needs to do it in secret. You know who the body was going to be.'

It feels as if the air around me has been snatched away.

'The king's,' I whisper.

'Indeed. The one way to ensure that the king's tomb is full of grave goods is to kill the king. That is what you got yourself mixed up in. But Panhese wasn't careful enough and I caught him, and since then I've been watching and waiting. I don't think he cared about the grave goods much, although a lot of priests work hand in hand with grave robbers. No. Panhese wanted to restore the old religion and the first thing he needed to do was bury the king according to the old rituals so he could be judged and sent to hell. Does that sound about right to you?'

I stare at him, too shocked even to nod. His words are

flying around in my head like big birds, but slowly they settle down into some kind of order. I don't care about Panhese. All I know is that Thutmose was plotting to kill the king. The Quiet Gentleman was plotting to kill the king. And they dropped me right in the middle of it without giving me any idea at all. A rage builds inside me.

'He said something . . .' I begin.

'Who said?'

'The Quiet Gentleman. He was passing himself off as Jatty, but his real name was Hannu. Him. The plan all went wrong because it depended on getting help from the high priest, Panhese, but he'd been arrested.'

'I see,' Mahu said. 'And what was the plan?'

'He was supposed to find the plans to the king's tomb and give them to us. That was the first thing. Next I had to claim that the head needed more work, important work, and get it out of the palace and back to the workshops.'

'With the plans for the tomb that Panhese had stolen for you in the box, presumably,' Mahu said. 'Clever. A bit risky because I might have thought to search it but . . .'

'No! Wait! It was better than that. The plans were to go *in* the queen's head, I think. Or something was . . . That's why the neck is so long.'

I stop to think. Is that it? I wish I wasn't so tired because my head feels empty, but at least when the memory does appear, there's nothing else to confuse it. The memory comes from the morning after I've finished working on the queen's head. I wander into the workshop and the Quiet Gentleman and Thutmose are looking at it. The Quiet Gentleman is saying something, but is shushed by Thutmose when I appear and I am so amazed by the way the head has been painted that I never follow it up. But what did the Quiet Gentleman say? Then suddenly it comes to me.

'"The stuff goes in; the plans come out,"' I repeat to Thutmose. 'The Quiet Gentleman was looking at the head and said, "The stuff goes in and the plans come out."'

'The stuff comes in . . . So, they were using the head to bring something into the palace as well. Interesting,' Mahu says, rubbing his bristly chin. And I notice that he looks tired. Not as tired as me, but tired. 'What stuff?'

'I don't know.'

'So we have a mystery.'

I can only agree.

'We need to take a look at that head,' Mahu says.

'I suppose.'

'Question: who brought it into the palace?' His eyes are on me now, very bright.

'Thutmose,' I say.

'Thutmose is not here. Question: who in this room brought it into the palace?'

'I did. But . . .'

Mahu interrupts me. 'I told you I was a simple man and I meant it. In my simple world, people take responsibility for their actions. You brought the head into the palace, so you must bring it to me. Think on how, boy. Think on it. And I'll think on it too. A word in the right ear might help.'

And he walks out of the room.

43. In which I meet the king

I'm allowed to sleep through that day and all the next night, and I awaken just after dawn. I lie for a moment, feeling heavy from so much rest, and try the door to my room. It opens. I'm not locked in. I see a door leading to a shady courtyard and head for it.

A man is curled up out there, asleep, but he wakes up as quickly as a cat and smiles at me without a hint of tiredness. He is wearing a lot of eye make-up and a really bad wig.

'There you are. I was just coming in to wake you. Got to make you look your best.'

'Who for?'

'Don't be silly. It's always good to look our very best.'

There's a basin of water and a washcloth that I use. While I'm washing, Painted Eyes is sharpening a razor by slapping it on a leather strap. I sit and he rubs oil into my scalp and shaves my head so that even the fine fuzz of bristles has gone and my scalp is as smooth as soapstone.

He draws dark rings around my eyes with kohl. While he works, he talks.

'What was your business with Mahu? He's a tough one. Caught me with my hand in the honeypot and the beating he gave me . . . Soles of my feet! My poor old back. I couldn't sit, couldn't lie, couldn't walk. I'd have spent the day standing on my head if I could. But I learned my lesson and I'll say this for Mahu: he's hard but fair. And the nonsense he has to put up with. Rushed off his feet, he is. Don't know when he gets time to sleep. Off to the desert one night, then the river. He also has his spies in town of course, listening out for plots against his Heavenly Hotness. Not that I can believe that anyone would plot against the king. How could they dare? Why would they want to? He gives us everything. You'll see when he talks to you.'

Listening to Painted Eyes is a bit like being pummelled so it takes a heartbeat or two for his last words to sink in.

'Mahu?' I say, not quite understanding.

'By the sun, no. The king; when the king sees you. What do you think all this fuss is about?'

'The *king* wants to see me? The king wants to see *me*?'

'In the Chamber of the Throne of the Greeting of the Sun. Careful you don't get scorched,' Painted Eyes says. He winks a heavily made-up eyelid at me, holds me at arm's length and views me critically. 'All done. Off we go. Whoops. No scent.'

He anoints my head with a different oil and rubs it in. I smell sweeter than one of the queen's attendants and I follow him through corridors that get wider and brighter.

It must be about his daughter and he's going to kill me. How did I think I was ever going to get away with it? We walk through a large hall, where the walls are painted in bright colours. Empty plinths along the walls, no statues here – just hot, busy-looking people. I'm grateful that Painted Eyes is hustling me along. It gives me less time to worry.

An audience chamber crowded with jostling, angry men. The air is getting hotter. Everyone is sweating. The guards are stripped down to simple loincloths, but even they are sweating. Down another corridor, the temperature rising with every step. A pillared throne room, an empty golden throne, glaring white walls. Soldiers standing to attention. It's an oven with one door in and one door out.

'The Chamber of the Throne of the Greeting of the Sun is just through there. Go on. Don't keep him waiting.' Painted Eyes is shooing me towards the exit. Heat is rolling from it in a torrent. 'You'll get used to it,' he says, backing away.

Sweat is streaming down my bare scalp and the oil is making my eyes sting. Satiah, the handmaiden, told me that there was no way out of the palace. You could only go further and further in. This is the very centre.

I force my way through the heat. The corridor turns

right, then back on itself, then right again. Now the light is growing and I am squinting against it. It's a force against me, a pressure. I screw my eyes tightly shut, but the light blasts through.

I almost trip on the steps. They are marked by sharp shadows. Squinting, sweating, weak, I climb into a small courtyard lined with metal that is as bright as the sun. I'm sure my skin is smoking. In the middle I can just make out the shape of a man on a throne.

The king.

Surrounded by light, blasted by light, he is an absence of light, but when I close my eyes, light becomes dark and he is a pale shape against the shimmering black. The heat is a screaming echo.

'Approach, boy,' he says. 'The sun is in me. Can you feel him? Can you feel the presence?'

'Yes, Lord.' I can feel nothing else. I'd kneel, but my knees would burn.

'His rays can fill me with his wisdom. Do you feel his wisdom?'

'Lord?'

'You work in his light. His light shows you the way.'

And the heat is baking all sense out of my head. 'I just see, Lord. Yes, the light shows me. Then I can do his work.'

A long pause. I think I'm about to faint.

'Good. You understand. In this palace, in this city, in this country, you are the only one to understand the new way. The new way of seeing is a new way of being. The sun is the sun. It is enough that he is the sun.'

'Yes, Lord.'

'We lay out his bounty under his eye so he can see. The people eat. When they eat, they eat his goodness and he is in them.'

'Yes, Lord.'

'Without the sun there is nothing. Everything comes from him, through me, to you. All goodness. All knowledge. All wisdom. Here in his city his will is done and soon the whole kingdom will be razed to the ground, brick by brick, stone by stone. The temples of the south and the tombs of the north will be no more. The pyramids of the Houses of Ascension will be no more and their stones will make new temples to the glory of the Aten. The temples of the south and the temples of the north shall be taken to pieces block by block and all his people will come to this city. All the world shall come to his city. ALL OF IT ALL THE TIME. **THERE SHALL BE NO WORLD BUT THIS CITY.**'

The words boom around the metal box, bouncing off the walls as harshly as the light.

'Yes, Lord.'

'You understand.'

'Lord, I need to ask you something,' I say.

His head tilts down. I feel his attention.

'The head of the queen. The Aten showed me how to

finish it. The Aten inspired me, but he has never seen it because the queen keeps it hidden away. The king should show it to the sun and the sun should judge whether it is worthy or not.'

There. I've asked. The silence gathers into something ominous.

'But the Aten sees all,' the king says. 'Whether the queen has it or the king means nothing to him.'

'But, Lord, I . . .'

'The Aten has spoken. Through me.'

He moves off. I stagger after him.

Painted Eyes is waiting for me in the throne room. He leads me back through the crowded audience chamber, down cool passageways back to my room where he pours cold water over my head, scoop after scoop, lays wet bandages over my eyes and then gives me juice to drink, pomegranate sweetened with honey.

And he never stops talking.

How did I find it? Was the king talking or was it the sun talking through him? Did I think it was hot? How the king stood it, only he knew, but he must have been chosen by the sun, by the Aten, because anyone else would have been burned to a crisp by now. Every day the sun shines, he's out there and now I've been chosen, he supposes I will have to get used to it too, but how did I find it . . .?

44. In which I have an unexpected visitor

The walls of my room are covered with painted scenes. In one, the king is setting out along the Royal Road in his chariot. The road is packed with well-wishers. In the next, he has spotted a lion. In another, the lion is writhing under his spear and in the last one, he is returning to the city with the lion strapped to the chariot. Needless to say, there are more cheering crowds.

A scratching at the door. It opens slowly and a small figure is standing there, all hunched up in a hooded garment made of sacking.

'More water for the young master,' it croaks. It's carrying an earthenware jug that's slopping water on the tiled floor.

'Thank you,' I say.

'And where does the little gentleman want it?'

'Er, anywhere.'

The figure staggers towards me. 'Here?' More water slops on to the floor. 'Here?' Even more. 'HERE?'

A huge spout of water slops from the jug and on to my lap. I leap to my feet. The water jug hits the ground, explodes, and the hunched little figure screams. With laughter.

'You!'

I back away as the princess throws back her hood.

'You should have seen yourself. Oh yes, just put it anywhere. Didn't you think you should help a poor old woman or have you grown too high and mighty now?'

'Yes. No. I mean, I should have helped her. You, I mean. But I haven't grown high and mighty.'

'So what are you doing here?'

'Why are you here?'

'Bored, bored, bored. So bored I might even go back to my mother. I can't play on the roof any longer.'

'And what does Your Highness want?' I ask.

She looks at me and pouts. 'I can't stand it when you cringe. I prefer it when you almost stand up for yourself. Should I make you angry? Is that what you need?'

I back away. 'What?' she says. 'Scared?'

'Yes.'

She sits down suddenly on the bed. 'I only came to thank my chamberlain. That's you, by the way. I've just appointed you.'

I watch her. Her mood has changed in the blink of an eye. Now she looks thoughtful. 'Of course I was very angry at first when we were caught because I thought you'd betrayed me. Then Mahu came to see me. He said he knew perfectly well that I'd been on the roof and his men only came after me because they were worried you might hurt me. I told him you wouldn't hurt me, would you?'

I shake my head.

'Good. I was right then. I asked whether you had betrayed me and he said you hadn't, even under torture. What he did do?'

'His men beat the soles of my feet, then they made me stand for hours without water.'

'Hmmm,' she says. 'He didn't pull out your fingernails or stick red-hot pins up your nose?'

'No.'

'That would have been a real test. Anyway, you've oiled your way into the king's affections, which is good because when he talks to you, you can report straight back to me.'

'But why does he want to talk to me?' I ask.

'The same reason my mother was interested in you. She thought you'd been sent by the king and so wanted to have a look at you. He knows you were the queen's favourite so he's curious too. Only I know the truth.'

Her eyes widen and she looks serious.

'What's that?' I ask. I'm suddenly worried that she's guessed I'm a tomb robber's apprentice.

'You've fallen in love with me!' she says.

I'm blushing. My face is as hot as the sun.

'It's true. It's true, isn't it? Poor baldy. Poor little chamberlain!'

'Stop it!' I shout and take a step towards her. She must sense that I mean it because she flinches. Something changes in her face.

'Ah! You're angry,' she says. 'I like that.'

'Don't tell the king,' I say. 'Don't tell anyone. And don't laugh about it.'

'Or what?' She plants her feet. 'Hah! Nothing. That's no good. It means you can't be bothered to be brave. You have to fight every step of the way here. You think you're the only one with troubles? Let me tell you mine.

'The king's having a feast tonight. There's a party from some northern country, Mitanni, coming and they're desperate for my father to marry their princess. What's that going to mean for me? I don't want some foreign princess hanging around. He'll ask me to be her friend or something, but I won't have it. And suppose he likes her? Suppose she tells him to send me away? You can't trust people here. You have to fight. Everyone has to fight.'

'But how?'

'The Mitanni people are barbarians and prudes. They think the way we go around half undressed is shocking and they can't even look at those statues of kings and queens if they've got bare tops.' She giggles. 'I've got a plan. I'm going to shock them into going back home and never coming back. And then I'll have the king all to myself and you and me can have some fun.'

'But, princess . . .'

'No discussion. Goodbye.'

45. In which I put my experience to use

As it turns out, I am going to the feast as the Holder of the Water Bowl for the Royal Fingers. The man who tells me this is some servant who is too superior to look me in the eye. He tries to tell me about my duties, but I know the feast could be an opportunity for me to get the queen's head so I don't really listen. Then I have a brainwave and interrupt him rudely.

'And will the queen be attended by her handmaidens?'

He shakes his head at my ignorance. 'Of course the queen will be attended by her handmaidens. It is a royal feast. The Mitanni are important allies of the state.'

'Thank you,' I say. 'That's all I wanted to know.'

He gives a stiff bow and leaves. I have dismissed him. That is what having an audience with the king does to a boy with no name's status.

It's a good hour before the feast begins. I watch the slaves who put out the tables argue with the slaves who put out the couches who argue with the slaves who will be bringing out the dishes. Then there are the dancing girls who argue with the musicians and they all argue with the acrobats who don't know if they're meant to be putting on a show when the guests arrive or after they arrive or during the feast.

Then the sun sinks behind the towers of the western gate, torches are lit, courtiers take their places on couches around the edge of the great hall. The musicians start playing – it sounds like cats being pecked to death by angry geese to me – and the dancing girls sway gently, like underwater reeds caught in the current.

The king arrives and as he does so a gasp rises up above the sound of the orchestra. He is walking into the courtyard with Meritaten by his side. Next comes Nefertiti, the queen, followed by their other children: Mekataten, Ankesenpaten, Setepenre and Tutenaten.

The music changes and the Mitanni appear at the great gate. They are swathed in thick woollen tunics and tall hats sit on the men's heads like chimneys. They march to their couches like suspicious peasants arriving at market: shoulders rolling, jaws jutting, eyes darting to left and right. At the sight of the half-naked courtiers, the men glower and the women put their hands over their eyes.

But if they are offended by us, I am disgusted by them. The hair on their heads is both long and tightly curled, like the coats of black sheep. It glistens with oil and hangs down their necks to below their shoulders. The men's beards are thick, curly and rough, oiled but not plaited or tamed in any way. It's as if the hair is boiling off their faces and falling off their chins like black foam.

The Mitanni take their places and, while wine is poured, the acrobats start their tricks. More agitation. Behind me, one of the servants sniggers. 'If they don't like the way the acrobats are dressed, they should go home,' he says. We can talk because the musicians are banging drums and cymbals as loudly as they can. 'Desperate, I call it.'

'What do they want?'

'They want one of their daughters to marry the king and the king needs the alliance.'

'Needs?' I ask.

'Of course. He's spent so much on the city, the army's gone to pot and the kingdoms to the north are getting ready to attack. That princess may not look like much, but she's brought a huge dowry and the Mitanni army's strong.'

'So the king . . .'

'The king nothing. It's all the queen's doing. Get the king busy with the Mitanni girl and then see what's what. But that princess – she's put the cat among the pigeons with those acrobats. You see the look on their faces? Priceless!'

Then the feast starts. Servants start carrying in dish after dish from the palace kitchens. Enough geese to feed an army – ostrich, antelope, ox and zebra. We know this because before each dish is presented, the servants come in wearing the skin or feathers of the dead beast and do a little animal dance.

The king hardly eats. His taster, a round man with sad eyes, takes a mouthful of every delicacy laid before the king, but for what purpose? The king will touch the food, bring it to his lips and then put it down again.

When he does this, I am ready with the finger bowl, and when I look up into his eyes, he is far away, as if he's taken poppy. He drinks the wine; the Mitanni only drink water. He picks at his food. They devour it as if it is the last meal they will ever have. He stares into the distance. They watch him with furious, wary eyes, apart from the princess who has been told to pout at him. A pause in the feast and now it's the dancing girls' turn to entertain us, but instead of dancing in front of all the guests, they're concentrating on the Mitanni and it's making them even more uncomfortable. When one of them dances right in front of the Mitanni princess, her father stands and pulls her away.

Our queen has seen what is happening and is on her feet. Her voice, shrill and furious, rises over the sound of the musical instruments. I manage to slip away and tap Sekmis on the shoulder. She's startled, but when I beckon she follows.

I move back, back, back, away from the king, until I'm standing against the palace wall in the shadow of a statue.

Sekmis, once so billowy and giggly, is looking tense and drawn. 'We need to talk,' I say. 'I . . .'

But she interrupts me. 'Satiah was killed yesterday. The queen accused her of spying for the king and Potipher drowned her in the pool. In front of all of us. She screamed! She splashed and then . . . It was awful. Terrible.'

'She was spying for the king?'

'No one knows for certain, but ever since you moved over to the king's side, the queen's gone mad with suspicion. She doesn't trust anyone.'

'But you were working for the princess, surely.'

'I can't get word out to her any longer. Everyone's being watched the whole time. Help me. Put in a word for me in the king's palace. You can do it. Please. I'm so scared.' Her voice breaks up into a sob.

My heart starts to beat a bit faster. This is going better than I could have expected.

'Help me and I'll help you,' I say. 'I want the queen's head. I need it back.'

'The head? You'll never get it. The queen has it with her morning, noon and night. She's obsessed with it. She stares at it and mutters, *Why? Why?* It's like you put a spell on it or something. There's no way I can get it.'

'What about when she's asleep?'

'It's by her bed.'

'I can't help it. That's the deal,' I say. 'I need it, and if you can get it to me, I'll put in a good word for you with the king.'

'And if I don't?' She looks desperate.

'The queen will hear that you were spying for the princess. Potipher will do the rest.'

'You'd do that to me?'

'It's the only way to survive here,' I say. 'I need the head tonight. I'll be waiting on the Bridge of Appearances at midnight.'

She stares at me and I force myself to hold her gaze.

'You little sneak,' is all she says. As she turns to leave, I catch a blast of her heavy, musky perfume and something else: the sharp, bitter tang of her terror.

I wait. Mahu moves out of the shadows on the other side of the statue.

'Well, young man,' he says, 'that was very interesting. And from what I could hear, you did well. You seem to be picking up the ways of the palace.'

'You heard everything?' I ask.

'As much as I needed. I'll tell the guards this side of the bridge what they have to do. Just you make sure you get your hands on that head. Now get back to your station.'

But the meal is over. Mitanni women are sobbing. Mitanni men are shouting. Courtiers are making soothing noises and the queen is looking stony.

The king rises and the court falls silent. He puts his hands out and I step forward with the bowl for him to dip his fingers. He looks down at me from a great height, the light from the torches playing in the strange hollows of his face.

'He comes with me,' is all he says.

And so I do.

46. In which I learn that if you don't move forward, you go back

We walk through the palace, taking the same route that Thutmose and I did when I first came here.

Nothing has changed: the same rooms, dark now, still smell of plaster and disuse. But everything has changed: tonight I am walking with the king.

We are followed at a discreet distance by courtiers and guards. The king doesn't say a word. He walks with long strides, his head swaying, and I am reminded of the nightmare vision of Anubis, the night Mahu tortured me. Perhaps the king really is a god.

I recognise the huge throne room I had to cross to reach the princess's room, but we leave by another door that leads to a staircase. Up it climbs, turning back on itself twice, and then we are on the roof, in the Chamber of the Throne of the Greeting of the Sun. The throne faces the desert and the night sky makes a fine ceiling. The moon is down. The night pulses with stars. I take my place on a stool to the right of the throne.

A night breeze carries the dry, stony tang of the desert, but I can smell wine coming from a tall jar. The king sits and clears his throat.

'The stars are jealous of the sun,' he says. 'They are

silver. It is gold. You know, before I was reborn, I built a temple for the old gods. I was Twice Born. I was born of my mother and I was reborn in the sun.'

'I was reborn in the water,' I say. 'I was put in a little reed boat and sent out into the river.'

'Then you are Twice Born too, but in the river. Perhaps that is why the Aten blesses you. He is jealous. He wants you for his own.'

More stars disappear on one side of the sky and more appear on the other. *The wheel turns, the wheel burns.*

'My father, Amenhotep, built palaces and temples. He fought wars and smote his enemies. He filled the temple coffers with gold until they groaned and burst and the gold spilled on to the floor in streams and in rivers. And what did he achieve? He made the priests rich and he died of toothache. There is no glory on this earth except for the burning glory of the sun.'

I wait for the sky to grow lighter, but if anything it gets darker.

'It is quiet now,' he continues. 'Sometimes I need the quiet so I do not hear the sun. He drowns me with his glory. Sometimes all I want to do is walk quietly in the field of the stars. Will you come with me, Twice Born?' the king says. 'Come with me and walk in the field of the stars?'

If I look up, I can picture two dark figures moving slowly across the countless points of light, the king and I, loose in the heavens. We're up there a long time, or at least it's a long time before the king talks to me again.

'Did you see them? Did you see the goddess Nut stretched across the sky like an arch? Did you see Osiris? Did you see the goddess Isis? Of course not. You saw stars and that is enough. Have you ever wondered how they hang there? Now you know that they hover like flies. They are a pestilence. It is good they are so far away.'

More of the pestilential stars buzz down to one horizon, and more buzz up from the other.

'When the sky is dark I do not have the sun inside my head. I spend my days listening to him. He smells loud. He sounds of hot stone. He booms. He screams. He whispers. He groans. His will must not be denied and he sees everything, Twice Born. Mahu talked about you to me. Did you know that?'

Mahu? *Mahu?*

He swallows.

'I have thirst.'

I get up. By the jug is a ladle and a wide cup. I fill the cup and hold it out to him, two-handed, my head bowed. He waits. I wait. He waits. Suddenly I realise what he is waiting for and drink, then hand him the cup.

'Good. Mahu tells me that my daughter trusts you,' he says suddenly.

'I . . . I don't know, Your Highness,' I answer, taken aback.

'I was not born to be a king. I had an elder brother. He

222

died. But before he died, I was free for a while and I knew trust. Do you trust her?'

'She told me not to, Lord.'

'Yes. She is right. I shall marry this Mitanni princess. It was clever of Nefertiti to see that. They want to honour us and our armies with gold. I should allow it. My hand in marriage is a gift and I am generous enough to give them that. We shall fight and bring back prisoners and they will build on the desert from here to the mountains and all the People of the Two Kingdoms will come here and the Land of the People of the Two Kingdoms will become the Land of the People of the Sun.'

'Yes, My Lord.'

'The princess does not want that. She is in error.'

'Yes, My Lord.'

A pause. 'Twice Born, when the Aten guides your hands, does his voice deafen you? Does it drown out all other sounds and all other thoughts?'

'No, Lord. It is so quiet, I cannot hear it.'

Another pause.

'If you had answered yes, I would have killed you.' He breathes in and out, as heavily as a cow for a long time. 'You must ask yourself a question.'

'Yes, Lord?'

'What is Mahu's interest in you? Think on it. You may go.'

*

As I run through the echoing palace all I can think about is Sekmis. How long was I with the king? Am I too late to meet her?

I think I know the way to the Bridge of Appearances, but as I cross the echoing space of the great throne room, I hear a sob, a dark shape blocks the doorway and a hand grabs me.

'Stop!' It's the princess. 'I was told you were with my father. What did he say? What is he going to do?'

'I . . . He didn't say anything.'

'Liar! He said things so you would hear and tell me. Did my plan work? Are the barbarians going to leave?'

'No,' I say. 'The king is going to marry the Mitanni princess. I think that was always going to happen. Your father needs allies. It's just . . . grown-up stuff.'

Her hands have been gripping mine and now she whips them away. 'I know grown-up stuff,' she snaps dismissively. 'It's called politics and ever since I could talk I've had to think about it. I'll have to go and live on the other side of the bridge with my mother and she hates me now! I thought I'd won, but she has and, if she's won, I've lost.' She grips me again tightly. By the whitening of her eyes in the darkness, I know she's opened them wide. 'You know she might have me killed?'

'She can't, and . . . I don't think she hates you and I don't think she wants to kill you.'

'Then she'll exile me to the north palace. If she does,

224

you must come with me. Say you'll come with me. Tell me! Promise me! I can't be on my own.'

'Surely it's not as bad as all that,' I say. 'If you and your mother made up . . .'

'You think there's anything to repair? That my mother wanted me by her side because she loved me? You don't know anything.' She breathes in then out. 'She wanted me there so the king didn't marry me. That is the only reason. And it always was.'

Of course I know and of course it was staring me in the face from the moment the princess first took me up on to the rooftops. She wanted one last moment of freedom before she became the king's wife. Before her father made his own daughter his queen.

I try and swallow back a growing feeling of sickness and nod. 'Up until I came here, I thought kings and queens and princesses were very different people from us, but now . . .'

'The same as you? What are you saying, slave boy?'

And even though I know the danger, I say: 'You want to be free. I want to be free. Maybe that makes us a little bit alike.'

'You don't understand. You don't understand anything. I can't ever be free. Either I have to marry my father have to go and live in the north palace where I mig well be dead. Unless . . .'

'Unless what?'

I know what she wants to say. I know she wants to say: Unless you come with me. Who knows? If she had said it, if she had asked again, maybe I would have gone with her.

But she didn't.

'You dare ask me?' she says. She gives a harsh little laugh. 'Slave boy dares to question a princess?'

'No,' I say. 'I don't. I have to go.'

'Go,' she says. But she holds my arm.

'Go now.' And she holds my arm even tighter.

'I can't just please you. I have to do this for me.'

I unpick her fingers and walk away.

47. In which I see an unexpected consequence of my actions

Mahu is waiting for me by the Bridge of Appearances.

'Late,' he snaps. 'Are you trying to ruin your own plan? You have to be here when she arrives. She won't trust anyone else.'

'... lost,' I say.

'... irl. This Sekmis. Does she have resolve?'

'... is coming off him in waves. For the first time ... et him he seems tense. I shrug. 'I know she's ... et away from the queen's court.'

'... you.'

'She told me that Potipher had strangled one of the other girls. Satiah.'

'Maybe the little idiot deserved to die.' Mahu says this so flatly that I am sure he knows. I gape at him.

'Is that all you can say?' I ask. 'Idiots die? Was she your spy? Don't tell me. I don't care.'

Then, through a window on the other side of the Royal Road, I catch movement – a flutter of white. I move to the bridge and hear the sobbing breath of someone running as if their life depended on it. The awful sound echoes down the empty corridors and then Sekmis appears, cradling a heavy bundle to her belly, her shoulders rising and falling as she struggles for breath.

'Show yourself,' Mahu says. 'Call her.'

I glance at him and a nagging doubt becomes a growing suspicion. I check for guards, but there are none, so I step out from behind a pillar and, from the other side of the bridge, Sekmis's face lights up. It seems to give her one last burst of strength. She's halfway across the bridge now and Mahu is holding me back until she's just a few paces away.

'Now,' he says, 'take the queen's head.'

I step up and take the weight of it. Sekmis yields gratefully, smiles and sinks to her knees, breathing hard.

'The queen never woke up,' she pants. 'After the feast she took the poppy drug to help her sleep. She'll be out for hours.'

Mahu is standing by Sekmis. 'Too late,' he agrees.

He reaches round her waist to help her up. And then I see the knife. It's in his hand and he's about to thrust it into her side.

I shout: 'No!'

He stops, but holds Sekmis closer. She starts to make a sound like a kitten, a faint mewing that's awful.

'You shouldn't have done that,' he says. 'Now she knows she's going to die, which is cruel.'

'But she helped us,' I say.

'By betraying the queen. How could I trust her after that?'

'You don't trust anyone,' I say. 'No one in the palace does. The only thing that matters here is power.'

'And she has none.'

'But I do,' I say. 'I have the head.'

'Oh dear,' Mahu says. 'Is that all?'

I step on to the bridge and hold the head out of the window where I first saw the king, the queen and the princess.

'Hurt her and I drop the head. Hurt me and I drop the head. You want to get your hands on it, don't you? Will it still be interesting if it's smashed? Suppose someone outside picks it up?'

Mahu lifts his arms and steps away from her. Sekmis collapses, sobbing.

'Sekmis, run and find the princess,' I say. 'She needs support and you'll know what to do. Go. GO!'

At heart, Sekmis must be a practical girl. She blinks at

me twice, then runs off. Mahu shows me his teeth in something that is not quite a smile.

'Satisfied?' he asks.

'Don't even think of hurting me,' I say. 'You still need me to talk to the king.'

48. In which a truth is revealed

I sit on the floor of Mahu's office, completely exhausted.

Mahu is on the other side of the room, issuing orders in a low voice to his guards. The head has been placed on a table. Under the high crown and the rearing cobra, the eyes stare at me coldly. My head, the queen's head . . . But why is it so important?

When I finished it, I thought it was beautiful. I thought it showed the queen as a real person and as a goddess, but now I know a bit more about people, it just seems fake. People can change; people die. This will always be as it is now: frozen in time, immobile, while people plot and scheme around it. It shouldn't be like that.

I rise from the floor and with a single, sudden movement I punch the head as hard as I can. It falls from the table and crashes to the ground.

Mahu looks up sharply. He holds his guards back with a simple gesture and smiles. 'Better now?' he asks.

I flap my hand which hurts badly. The head lies on its side, missing an eye now, the rearing cobra snapped off, chips of painted plaster scattered on the floor. I shake my head. I sit again. And then, and then . . . I see something.

The queen's neck is very long and elegant and is fixed to the stand by a sort of lug. When I punched the head, I knocked it off the stand and right now I am staring into the hole at the base of the neck. And I can see something in there.

I reach inside. My fingers tell me they are touching an object made of wood, like the turned handle on the lid of a box. I manage to prise it out: a small, well-made wooden cylinder.

'And there we have it,' Mahu says. 'The cause of all the trouble. Did you never think?'

I shake my head and hand over. It sounds hollow when Mahu taps it. The top unscrews.

'See that?' Mahu asks. Inside the cylinder is a fine white powder. 'That's why getting the head into the palace was the really important thing. This is the heart of the matter. You thought you were bringing the head into the palace to help you smuggle the plans out. You didn't know you were smuggling something in. Enough poison to kill a herd of elephants, let alone a king, I would say. It's the last piece of the puzzle.'

'You make sure the king's tomb is full of grave goods by killing the king,' I say.

'But how do you kill the king? Well, there's the answer.'

'You don't sound very surprised,' I say.

'Oh, nothing surprises me,' Mahu says flatly. Then something must occur to him because he says with sudden passion: 'I should have killed that girl. She brought the poison to the king's palace.'

'But she didn't understand what she was doing. She's innocent.'

'You're missing the point. She might have claimed credit later. He's not popular, you know.'

'But how . . . how could she claim credit for something you prevented? Unless . . . Oh no,' I say. 'Oh no.'

'Say it.'

'Unless the poison *does* kill the king.'

'Good boy,' Mahu says.

'But you said you were loyal to him. You said . . .' I run out of words.

'I said I was loyal to the kingdom and I don't know how much more it can take. Does he really think he can move the entire country here? To this dry, stinking waste of mud brick and sand? Is that why he's forming an alliance with the Mitanni? Will their gold turn the whole country into a prison where we all worship the sun? Isn't that what he told you?'

'Yes,' I say. 'It just sounded different when he said it.'

'We cannot let him do it,' Mahu says. 'It will not work. There is no power on earth that could achieve that.'

'It's you then? It's you that wants to kill the king?'

'I am loyal to the Land of the Two Kingdoms which is being slowly killed by his madness.'

'So what are you going to do about it?' I ask.

'The question is what are *you* going to do? You will join the king in the Chamber of the Throne of the Greeting of the Sun. You will put the poison in his wine and he will drink it. It is a simple thing and you will do it.'

'Or?'

'This is your choice. Do as I tell you and the kingdom will reward you for your services. You will save yourself, save your sister and be free. If you refuse, you will die and your sister will die. Horribly. I caught you red-handed as you took delivery of the poison that you brought into the palace. There will be a trial. The king will think you betrayed him; the princess will think you betrayed her; the queen will not know what to think. You will be executed in such a way to discourage other people from trying to kill the king. If you are lucky, you will be unconscious before you are staked out in the sun. If you are unlucky, you will feel the sun cooking you to death.'

He pauses.

'You are so very close to death; you are so very close to freedom. Choose wisely. Do the right thing.'

I stand.

'I'll do it,' I say. It doesn't seem to be worth adding that I don't seem to have a choice, but I say it anyway.

'Of course you will,' Mahu says. He hands me the little wooden box and his guards take me away. I leave him looking at the ruined head. He is shaking his head and clucking sadly. He stoops. Picks it up. Puts it back on the table. Stares at it some more.

49. In which I make a choice

I have the light-headed feeling of someone who hasn't slept in a very long time: dreamy yet knife-sharp.

The way to the throne room seems to be lined with guards. Mahu's men, I'm assuming. They are in every doorway and along every corridor. When I have to cross a great hall, two guards lead me across it, three sets of footsteps echoing off the walls. Mahu is leaving nothing to chance. I feel half like a prisoner and half like the most important person in the world.

Which, in a sense, I am. At the dawn of this day, the world revolves around mud boy.

I walk through the corridor then climb the steps to the Chamber of the Throne of the Greeting of the Sun.

'Twice Born,' the king says. 'You have come to greet the living sun.'

He is a shape that talks. In the moonlight I can see the low range of mountains that bounds the desert to the east of the city.

Has he stayed here all night? Is that dew on his copper skin? Does he think it's odd that I am here again?

No, because he talks.

'We talked about trust last time,' he says. 'Now I must ask: can I trust you?'

My mouth goes dry and my hands start shaking. I swallow.

'Yes, Lord,' I say.

I look at the sky. Dawn. Night dissolving on the jagged horizon.

'Tell me what you see,' the king says.

'Desert. Sky. A line of mountains.'

'And?'

'There's a notch in the line of the mountains,' I say. The sun is rising behind it. It's like a cup filling with light,' I say.

'Indeed. The notch is like the sign for horizon that the scribes use. I saw it once, before I was reborn. I was on a boat. It was dawn. I was travelling from the great city of the south to the great city of the north. I was leaving behind one city full of greedy priests and going to another city full of greedy priests. They named me a god in the same way a man names his child, so he can call it; so it will come when he calls. They named me a god so they could own me, like a farmer brands his cattle, so I could be theirs. And then I saw the sun rise in that notch. I saw the sun *on* the horizon, I saw the sun *in* the horizon.

I saw this was my new beginning. The City of the Sun's Horizon. It is my beginning and it will be my end. Here, I named myself. Once I was Amenhotep, *Amun is Satisfied*; now I am Akenaten, *Effective for the Sun*. Bring me wine, Twice Born. It is time to drink.'

He is massively calm, like an ox. I think of all those cattle I saw slaughtered in the temple, how the first, swift chop that killed them dropped them to their knees, as if they were praying.

Now the mountains are rimmed with light; the little notch is spilling gold. I fill the king's cup with wine using a ladle. I put the ladle down and take out the tube of poison. This is it. This is the moment that the sun is reborn. I have my back to him and he cannot see what I'm doing.

I turn. The rings glint on the king's fingers as he reaches out to take the cup from my shaking hand.

'Before you drink, Lord, I would like to prove that your trust in me is justified,' I say.

I drink. The wine is rich and sweet. Its vapours rise into my head and warm it.

'You did not need to do that,' the king says. 'And still you live.'

He takes the cup and he drinks. My legs give way and I collapse. We wait as the sun clears the mountain and starts to shine upon the world.

'You knew?' I say.

'The Aten sees everything,' he says. 'Even into Twice

Born's heart. But I would like to hear why you did not kill me.'

'Mahu said I would be free if I put the poison in the wine,' I said. 'But I do not know what freedom means any more. Ever since I left home, people have been telling me that if I don't do what they ask I will die, but if I do what they want I shall be free. But I can't be free like that. I can't be free if I am on their path; if I can only do what they want. When I spoke to the princess earlier, she said she would never be free, and so . . . if she can't be free, how can I be?'

'And?' the king sounds almost human.

'Tell the Aten that if I couldn't be free, I didn't want to be a killer as well. Not killing the king was my decision. So I could be free. Even if Mahu kills me.'

'The Aten knew this,' the king said. 'The Aten sees all.'

'Yes, Lord.'

'Did Mahu really think that he could plot against me without me knowing? Did Thutmose? Mahu will be killed. Thutmose will be killed and all his craftsmen. His workshops will be buried. All memory of him will be erased. The head of the queen will be buried with him and a curse will be placed on it so that if it is ever found again, it shall be put on display, a thing to be gawped at like a dancing girl on a street corner.'

'The guards,' I say. 'They're Mahu's men. They're in the throne room, just outside.'

236

'No. Mahu thought they were his men and, if I had died, then perhaps they would have followed him, but not now. Not now they hear me talking. The king is still the king.'

'And the workshops? When are you going to destroy Thutmose's workshops?'

'The soldiers will have gone already. I think; they act.'

'And their orders?'

'To take the head of the queen and leave it in the workshops. Then destroy the workshops. To find everyone in the workshops and kill them. All of them.'

'But Lord,' I say. 'My sister is there. I must save her.'

A pause that stretches and stretches. A sparrow lands on the roof and starts to peck at some invisible speck of food.

'If you want to save her, you must run,' the king says.

50. In which I see the destruction of Thutmose's workshops

I don't remember running from the palace. It's as if time collapsed and the city folded like a sheet of papyrus. One second I'm with the king, the next I'm standing outside Thutmose's workshops, my lungs heaving and my legs weak.

A ring of soldiers is surrounding the area and there are

sounds coming from inside that I don't want to hear. Shrieks and grunts and thuds. I'm too late. I scream that I'm allowed in, that the king has told me to save the people I love, but of course it makes no difference. They've been told to kill everyone inside the workshops and that's what they're doing.

I'm still yelling, 'Stop it! Stop it!' when someone grabs me and pulls me away. It's Sethi. He's grey-faced and shocked.

'Where have you been?' he says. 'Everyone said you'd been taken up by the queen, then by the king. Have you come from the palace? Can you stop them?'

'I can't do anything,' I say and then a howl gathers in the pit of my belly and screams from my mouth. 'IMI! IMI! Where are you?'

Sethi's holding me, trying to calm me down. I take his shoulders and shake him. He feels like loose bones in a thin sack. 'How did you get away? What happened?"

'I was asleep on the roof. I heard them coming and ran off.'

'And you didn't warn anyone? What about Imi?'

'I . . .'

A scream comes from the kitchens and I tear myself away from him. They're killing the cooks and the serving girls. I hurl myself at the cordon of soldiers again and am hurled back. I do it again and again until I'm too hurt and tired to do it any longer.

Then they start to bring the bodies out. I recognise some of the craftsmen and some of the minders. Thutmose is about the third one out. He has shrunk so he just looks like a little dead monkey. Then the cook's assistant. Then the cook. I feel cold and start to shiver. The cart is full; they're laying out the bodies on the ground and people are coming to stare. I hate them with a passion but then I see a woman in the crowd collapse and start to wail and I realise that I'm not the only person to lose a loved one.

'That's it!' A squat guard with a scarred face and blood dripping off his sword comes out of the workshops.

'Smash the roof then push the walls down,' the captain says.

What do I do? If I shout that they've missed two people, they'll send soldiers in and hunt them down and kill them. If I do nothing, they'll push the buildings in on top of them. When no one is looking, I slip in and run through the rooms, hissing, 'Imi! Imi!'

I look in all the places I know she would hide – in cupboards and under benches – but she's not there. I try to ignore the pools of blood, the overturned chairs. In the kitchens, bread is burning in the ovens; she's not hiding there. There are soldiers up above, smashing through the roof. They've put huge battens of wood outside the doors and roped them to oxen. When the oxen pull, the battens will drag the mud walls down. I run out as walls collapse in clouds of thick, smoking dust.

Outside, Sethi is waiting for me. 'What did you run inside for?' he asks.

'I thought they must be hiding. I thought I could find her.'

'You ran off before I could say: they left last night. Your sister and the one you call the Quiet Gentleman.'

'What?'

'In the middle of the night. It was hot and I couldn't sleep. The place had gone mad. Thutmose was ordering people to do this and that; he was trying to get hold of carts and go into the desert, at least that's what I thought. They forgot to lock me in and I went up on to the roof.'

I grab him by the arms. 'Where did they go? What were they doing?'

I'm too frantic to feel relieved.

'They had water. They were heading out into the desert.'

'Which direction?'

But I don't really need him to show me. His arm is pointing straight at the notch in the mountains; the place the king said was his beginning and his end. The place where his tomb has to be. The Quiet Gentleman must have set off with Imi, thinking that the plot to kill the king was going to succeed.

For the first time since I left the palace, I am not in a state of despair. I'm just very, very tired.

'I've got to sleep,' I say. 'Then I have to follow my sister into the desert.'

51. In which I head into the desert

I sleep all day as I know I can't set out before nightfall. My life has suddenly narrowed down so far that I don't even have decisions to make any more. All I must do is cross the desert and find my sister. In the palace I couldn't see where I was or where I was going. I was blind, relying on luck and instinct to survive. Here, on the edge of the desert with the city behind me and Sethi waving me goodbye, all I have to do is walk.

It's hard at first. There are rocks and low bushes, but once my eyes adjust the stars give off just enough light to show me where I'm going. Then the moon rises and its stark light throws up deeper shadows. Off to my left I see dark parallel lines snaking off towards the mountains.

Ruts. Cart tracks.

The ruts are new – wind-blown sand has not blurred their edges and they're heading as straight as an arrow for the notch in the low mountains ahead of me. I'm sure they are heading for the town in the desert, the secret town that the Quiet Gentleman found where the tomb builders live.

I'm making no noise. The sandals I was given at the palace are soft and better designed for shuffling across the polished floors of the great halls than walking on bare earth, but out here they keep my footsteps quiet.

I am a ghost in the moonlight. I can hear the skitter of the little desert mice as they search for food, the cry of an owl, the bark of a dog, the clink of metal on stone and distantly, very faint, the groan of wood on wood.

I stop and step back from the track. The clink was in front of me. The wooden groaning is coming from behind. Guards in one direction, a cart in the other? The cart is coming from the city and guards are waiting for it?

I hunker down and wait, counting my breaths to help make the time pass. Just as I reach two hundred the creaks become a black shape twenty paces or so down the track. But it's not one cart, it's a convoy. I move about ten paces from the track and walk alongside it, watching out for boulders and gulleys. I can hear the carters talking to each other in low voices.

'What's that flap on at the palace? Heard there was trouble.'

'Someone said old Mahu got too big for his boots and the king strangled him.'

'Mahu? He's a wily old fox. He wouldn't get caught. It was the queen. A palace coup. I'm telling you, we won't be seeing her ride out with His Royal Highness ever again.'

'Shh. Getting close to the guards. Here we go.'

'That's far enough! Identify yourselves.' The voice is officious and confident. Typical city guard.

'Who do you think? Nubian raiding party? It's supplies for the builders. One cart flour and lentils; one cart assorted vegetables; one cart water,' the man answers.

The convoy creaks to a halt. I creep closer.

'Less of your lip. Extra security tonight. Warning of a raid.'

'It's to scare you,' the carter says. 'Keep you on your toes. There's trouble in the city.'

'That's as may be,' the guard says. 'But you'll run into a patrol. Password's Jackal.'

'Nice. We'll be on our way then.'

The convoy creaks on. I skirt round the guards then get back on to the road, this time following about twenty paces behind the carts.

But perhaps it's too easy walking behind them. Perhaps that's why I'm walking more and more slowly. Perhaps that's why I stop when I see a shooting star out of the corner of my eye and look for another. Perhaps that's why I breathe in and feel happy and relaxed for the first time since I saw the Quiet Gentleman's dust cloud from the top of the pyramid.

Vast stillness. I stop walking. Utter silence. Just me and the stars and nothing else.

The carts! I can't even hear them! And the track! How did I get off the track?

There seems to be a low hill between me and the mountains so I can't see them. Which direction do I take? The hill. If I can get to the top of the hill I'll be all right. If . . .

One minute it's me and my panic; the next it's sweat and leather and rough hands grabbing me and lifting me off my feet.

'This ain't no desert fox,' a voice says. 'This ain't even a little stray goat. This, lads, is a boy.'

I writhe and bite until I'm cuffed across the face, then with my head singing and a hand holding on to my ear, I subside.

'Who's this then?'

'I got lost,' I say.

'You got very lost. You know you're in a security zone? Very far into a security zone, so how you got past the other patrols I don't know, unless you were trying very hard.'

Words come from nowhere, like flies. 'I was with the carts,' I gabble. 'But I dropped back to . . . do my business. Then I lost them, I don't know how. I must have panicked.'

'What carts?'

'Taking supplies to the builders' town. One cart of flour and lentils, one of mixed vegetables and one of water. My dad'll kill me if he finds out I got lost, kill me dead. Where are they? Can you help me?'

'Steady on. What's a kid doing in the convoy?'

'My mother died and Dad doesn't like leaving me on my own,' I say. 'We came here looking for work, but all that happened was my mother got sick and he ended up driving a cart. He's a carpenter. He thought he'd . . .'

'All right, all right, spare me. Every poor bastard in the city's got a sob story to tell. See that jag in the cliffs? Head in that direction and you could even cut them off before they reach the builders' town.'

Then, as I turn to set off, he says: 'Hold on.'

I stop dead and wait for a heavy hand to slam down on my shoulder.

'What's the password, kid?'

'Jackal,' I call over my shoulder and then I'm off.

I crash into a thorn bush and then down a gulley they forgot to tell me about, but I reach the road after not very long and listen. I can hear the carts creaking so it seems that they're not too far in front of me. The road must have detoured round the river bed and I have managed to cut off a corner.

I keep closer this time and it's nearly dawn when the carts stop at the town of the tomb builders.

All I can see are high walls, but I can smell woodsmoke as the fires are lit for breakfast and hear a cock crow close by. Even though this place is in the middle of nowhere, it all feels familiar because I'm smelling the smells and hearing the sounds of home.

I'm very tired. Homesickness twists a spear in my guts and I'm drawn to the gates where the carts are waiting. But torches have been lit so a scribe can make a note of the provisions that are delivered and there's no way I can get inside the town.

Even if I did, what then? Could I beg? It's not a big place. Everyone must know everyone else and I'd probably stand out like a sore thumb with my shaved head, made-up eyes and soft, ornamental sandals. No, they'd put me on the next cart back and I'd be no nearer finding the Quiet Gentleman and Imi.

At some point in the night my sandals have worn through and my feet are bleeding, so I limp away, find a rock with a hollow underneath it, curl up and fall asleep.

52. In which I learn something surprising about myself

I'm swimming in darkness, but someone's managed to slip a huge hook through my ear and is trying to drag me up into the light. I fight. I want to hide in the darkness. It gums my eyes together and keeps me asleep.

Then I'm awake with a gasp and the tiredness is sluiced off me by the cold shock of panic. I'm being poked in the ear by a sharp stick and at the other end of it there's a frowning face.

I struggle up, or try to, but the stick pushes me back against the rock. Voices jabber and hawk: no language I've ever heard. It sounds like camels trying to be sick. I sit still.

'Boy from city?'

I nod. The man has a thatch of very black, thick hair and quick, intelligent eyes.

'Bad place hiding. Come.'

He holds out a hand and I surprise myself by taking it. His companion is startled when I come out into the light. The other man looks at me closely then nods.

Crouching low, we work our way behind the boulder before dropping down into a dry river bed. A hundred paces on, a large rock has fallen into it, hemmed by thorn bushes. The man carefully takes a branch and lifts it, making a crawl space. Beyond is a dark hole.

'Hide there,' he says. 'Safe. Soldiers looking.' He gives me an enormous wink. 'You hiding. Go!'

I don't see that I have any choice. I wriggle under the thorn bush, through the hole and find myself in a cave. There's enough light to make out a rough mattress, a large jug and a wooden box. In the jug is water and I drink it. In the box is stale bread and I eat. Then I have a proper look around.

The walls carry the marks of chisels so it's man-made, but over these people have scratched other things. Some of the marks are the familiar pictures of our language; others are strange, spidery squiggles. People have drawn pictures, some of them very rude. Tunnels run out of the cave in three different directions. They are dark, too dark to explore, and smell of stone and damp.

I lie down and try to sleep, but no matter how I wriggle I can't get comfortable. Earlier I was sleeping under a rock; now that I have a roof over my head and a mattress under me, it seems that all I can feel are lumps. There's one in particular near my head. I reach round to see if it's a pebble I can move, but as soon as my fingers touch it I know what it is.

I sit up and roll the mattress back, my heart pounding. It's one of the small mud figures I made for Imi, a desert fox all curled up with its sharp little nose tucked under its tail. She must have been here with the Quiet Gentleman! I hug the tiny animal to me and feel hope for the first time in weeks. We're out of the city. I'm on her trail. Surely I will find her soon.

The two men who found me reappear a short while later carrying small lamps. They've brought three other people with them: two men, both older than them, and a boy of about my age.

They talk together, then the man who woke me says: 'Why are you here?'

I take a deep breath. 'I'm following a big man and a small girl,' I say. 'I know . . .'

'What is your name?' the man interrupts.

I shake my head. 'Some people call me mud boy,' I say. 'The Queen called me Boy Who Did Not Bow To The King. The king called me Twice Born.' I shrug.

A long discussion. The man breaks off to say: 'The boy

thinks you are cracked.' He taps his head. 'Anyone who thinks that the queen calls him one thing and the king calls him another must be mad. But I tell him that you might have a story to tell.'

'Please,' I say, 'I know my sister was here. She left this. I made it for her.'

One of the other men is wagging his finger. 'Not your sister.'

'But it must be. She was here. This . . .'

'She was here, but she is not your sister. You are not . . .' He says a word that I do not understand, then turns to the first man for guidance.

'We call your people foreigners,' he says. 'We call ourselves the Chosen People. We think you are one of us. Look!'

And they push forward the boy. He crouches opposite me and screws his face up. It takes a second to realise that he is imitating me. I frown. He frowns. I look away. He looks away.

I say: 'Stop it.'

He says: 'Stap et.'

He doesn't only have my face, he has my voice as well. 'What's going on?' I ask. 'Who are you?'

'Many, many years ago we were brought to the Two Kingdoms as slaves from a land to the north. Ever since then we have lived here, worked here and dreamed of going home and now we have the chance.'

They tell me that a big man and a small girl were here yesterday, running from the city. The man was very tired but the girl was all right and they think he must have been carrying her a lot of the way. They wanted to know about the tomb and they paid good money for the information. One other thing: if a boy turned up looking for them, the tomb builders were to help him.

'So they are there now?'

'We told them: "It is dangerous. The tomb is finished and the king will be visiting it very soon to look at it. If he catches you there, you will be killed." But the big man just said: "Oh, the king is coming to the tomb but he won't be killing anyone." What can we do? If this man wants to kill himself, let him kill himself, and he paid us well. But you should be careful. You shouldn't go there in the night. There are lions and jackals in the desert.'

But the talk of the king just makes me more determined. I try to be patient and thank them, but say that I really have to go. They give me a lamp and tell me that one of the tunnels leads to the mouth of the valley where the king's tomb lies.

53. In which I take a long walk in the dark

There are guards at the mouth of the valley and tomb diggers have made these tunnels so they can avoid them when they want to. It's a long crawl on my hands and knees and by the time I reach the end, the little lamp they have given me is guttering.

On either side of me, the walls of the rocky valley rear up, rough and steep. Its mouth is deep and dark and somewhere behind me stands the line of guards.

A day has passed in the cave and darkness has settled thickly in the valley by the time I reach it, but the path is smooth, worn down by the feet of the builders passing from their village to the tomb and back again week after week, month after month, year after year.

I sense more than see the valley walls narrowing on either side of me. At first my shuffling footsteps echo off the walls, then the rock seems to swallow the sound. On I walk. Above me stars appear in the jagged slice of black sky. The ground rises and sweeps round to the right. The builders didn't tell me about this. I stop.

Is it my imagination or have I picked up an echo?

I turn around. 'Hello?'

'. . . lo.'

My voice returns to me – at least I hope it's my voice.

My fear creates a long-legged, yellow-toothed, fat-bellied thing stalking down the valley behind me. I'm scared that the thing might answer and I keep quiet after that, my scalp prickling at every sound. I back towards the edge of the valley, but where I expect to find rock I find nothing.

The tomb builders told me to look for a narrow gulley hidden by an outcrop of rock that cuts through the cliff as if a giant has hacked it with an axe. This must be it! I walk down it, almost blind. Where it turns, I will find the tomb.

After I've been walking carefully for a few minutes, I sense an even thicker darkness in front of me. This must be where the gulley turns again. I'm walking cautiously down the left-hand side, my hand on the wall, when I stub my toe. I bend down. I haven't walked into a random rock, but a dressed stone block. On the other side it drops away to nothing and then my hands find steps, cut down into the rock.

'Hello,' I call again in a hoarse whisper.

Nothing. On all fours, I take a few steps down. The smell of cut stone and dead air wraps around me. This whole story started with Imi disappearing into a tomb: is this how it's going to end?

I was brave then and I have to be brave again and call into the darkness.

'Imi, are you there?'

Silence. I'll have to go in. I back down all the way, sensing as my head sinks below the level of the earth. The steps are steep and rough. I count twenty and then forget to count any more; the sense of rock pressing in around me is so terrifying.

I remember that a stonemason in Thutmose's workshops told me that the stone he carved had been waiting underground for as long as the earth was old, patiently holding up mountains until men came and chipped it free and brought it into the light. All that stone above me, below me and on either side: what does it think about this tunnel carved into it? I know: it wants to crush it. I think I can hear the rock groan and creak. I know the Aten has burned up the old gods in the sky, but what about the old gods of stone? What of them?

The darkness is as thick as felt. It presses on my eyes. I keep my hand on the wall, running it along the chisel marks. Then the wall stops suddenly and turns right. Is this the main tunnel turn or is it a side tunnel? I know the stories about the old tombs: that they have traps and hidden doorways. Suppose this is a trap of some sort. Touching the wall with one hand, I reach out into the darkness. It grasps nothing. My heart thumps in my ears.

'Imi!' I call again. 'Imi?'

What if she isn't in the tomb at all? Suppose she and the Quiet Gentleman are waiting outside?

And then I see a light. Or rather it isn't a light, just a lessening of the darkness. I do that trick of looking at it out of the corner of one eye, then turning my head and using the other eye. It doesn't move. It's real and outside my head. I step out into the darkness and, after two paces, find the far wall so I continue on my way.

The light grows. I can see it flickering on the walls now and then I find it: a little oil lamp set into a niche in the wall, out of my reach. Just beyond it, more steps, even steeper this time, arrow down.

'Imi!'

'I'm here!'

She sounds so close. I almost run down the steps. The tunnel carries straight on with another entrance to my right.

'Where are you?' I call and take a step.

'Stop right there!'

The order clangs round my head. I stand statue-still.

'Look down.'

There is no floor. My heart flops into my belly. I almost fall forward into the pit.

Flint sparks blaze. Another lamp flickers into light.

'Are you alone?' the Quiet Gentleman asks.

I nod. 'Yes. But maybe not for long. Mahu is dead. Thutmose is dead. The king is still alive. What are you doing down here? Why is Imi down here?'

He ignores my questions.

'What happened?' His voice is as heavy as mud.

'The king's still alive!' I say. 'I've come to get Imi!'

'How . . . what?' It's the first time I've seen him taken by surprise.

254

'There's no time to waste! The king will be here soon!'

'And you know this how?'

'Because I've just escaped from the palace to help you! Come on!'

He closes his eyes. Shakes his head. Breathes out then steps back into the shadows. I hear scraping and he works a ladder across the pit.

'Hold it your end,' he says. 'I'm sending your sister over first.'

She clambers over on all fours while the Quiet Gentleman holds the lamp up high to light her way. She doesn't falter. She keeps her eyes on me, even as the ladder dips in the middle, and then she's over and she jumps up into my arms like a little monkey, and I squeeze her and she squeezes me until we are out of breath.

'Touching,' the Quiet Gentleman says. 'But could you just keep your foot on the ladder your end? This is not as easy as it looks and I have to make it across quickly.'

It doesn't look easy at all. He has a heavy bag slung over his shoulder and is holding the lamp in one hand which means he can only really cross standing up, stepping from rung to rung and balancing.

'Are you sure you can make it?' I ask.

'Yes,' he grimaces, three paces in.

'Do you need that bag? It looks heavy.'

He is about a quarter of the way across, halfway to the middle, and the ladder is already bending like a bow.

'Please stop talking,' he says.

The length of ladder over the edge is about a hand's breadth long, but as the Quiet Gentleman reaches the middle of the pit the ladder begins to slip under my feet. I can see sweat on his brow and he takes a moment, at the point of greatest danger, to pause. The ladder stops flexing and begins to creak. The end under my feet slips again. Next to me, I hear Imi draw a breath that she doesn't let out.

'I know you used me,' I say. 'I know about the queen's head. I know it was used to bring poison into the palace to kill the king. It all came down to me in the end. I could have killed the king, but I didn't.' I take one foot off the ladder. 'Did you think I would live?'

'Yes,' the Quiet Gentleman says through gritted teeth. 'I always thought you would.'

'But it went wrong.'

'And yet you lived.'

'But not because of you!' I say.

'Because of you. And that's a better way, isn't it?'

'You used me. I should kill you.'

'Instead of the king? Why not? I've lost everything. The tomb builders drive a hard bargain. Their price for helping me get into the tomb was that golden statue of Hathor. What a waste!'

He takes another step, and another.

'Wait,' I say.

'Enough,' he answers. 'You still need me.' He lifts his head to meet my eye and suddenly the ladder is gone, the light is out and there's a harsh clatter of wood hitting rock. I have an image seared on to my eye in the darkness of the Quiet Gentleman launching himself into the darkness, his arms outstretched, his hands grasping for the edge of the pit, his fingers hooked and ready to grip.

A thump. A groan. But it's not the sound of a man hitting the bottom of a hole; it's the sound of palms slapping against the wall of a pit, a grunt and the heavy breathing of a man hanging by his fingertips from a slippery ledge of rock in the pitch-black of a tomb.

Imi is on her hands and knees, scrabbling to feel where he is, but it's me that finds him. He is hanging on by two finger joints, trying to get a purchase on the slippery rock ledge. Failing.

I try to grab his wrists, but they are too thick and smooth. His tunic is too loose. Then my fingers touch the strap of his bag. Without thinking I grab it, yelling at Imi to hold my waist and pull. I feel the bite of the strap and throw myself backwards, feet slipping on the floor, my shoulder muscles screaming.

And he doesn't fall. After a while I hear the soft thump of the Quiet Gentleman heaving himself up as the strap goes slack in my hand.

In the distance there's a mighty, grating roar and then silence floods back stealthily.

'That,' the Quiet Gentleman says, 'was the sound of the tomb being sealed.'

54. In which I state the obvious

'We've got to get out of here!' I shout.

'Stay!' The Quiet Gentleman's voice carries enough force to stop me. 'If the tomb's completely sealed, you'll never escape. If it isn't, they'll kill you as soon as you stick your head out and then seal it anyway.'

'But who did it? The tomb builders?'

'I don't know why they would. I had a deal. I paid them.'

'Perhaps, now the king's alive, they think the deal's off.'

'It doesn't feel right. This was always part of the plan: to hide in the tomb and break out with the treasure, but there was meant to be back-up, support, lamps, ropes . . .'

'What's in that bag?'

'Tools to help us break out once the tomb is sealed.'

'So we're all right!'

'No. We have a problem. There's only one place we can break out. The tomb builders marked it, but without the light I can't find it.'

'How . . . how does tomb robbing work?' I ask. 'What was meant to happen?'

There's the sound of the Quiet Gentleman rolling on to

his back. 'People like me, tomb robbers, would bribe anyone involved in making a tomb to tell us where it was. Then we might overpower the guards and break in the front way or tunnel in through the side secretly. This tomb is different. It's got a narrow front and mountain above it, behind it and to either side. Now, the guards are no fools. They would count all the workers in during the day and count them out at night, so the tomb builders would have to be clever. All it would take is one extra person, smuggled in, to spend the night here secretly.'

'Doing what?'

'Tunnelling out to make a second entrance, a secret one. They'd work through the night and the next day, then leave while another worker took their place – the guards don't count the number of workers inside the tomb, only the numbers going in and out, and of course to them all the workers look the same. In the end, the tomb has two entrances. The main one which is blocked at the funeral, and the secret one that they disguise with mud bricks and plaster. So I hide in the tomb, get buried with the king and then, when the tomb's sealed, find the tunnel and hack my out of it to open up the secret door. Then we all rob at leisure. Gut the place.'

There seems to be nothing to say. The gulf between how things are and how they are meant to be is too wide to think about. The darkness has a soft pressure that seems to be increasing, minute by minute. The only sounds are the ones we make ourselves and they seem to be getting louder. Fear comes on me like a thief. It steals all the brave bits and replaces them with a cold and silence.

I lie on my back, closing my eyes and opening them. If I close them and scrunch my fist into my eyes, I can see coloured dots. In other words, I can see more with my eyes closed than with my eyes open.

I feel Imi move beside me. 'What's happening?' she whispers. 'The Quiet Gentleman said we were going home very soon.'

I pause before answering, deciding that a lie is the best option.

'We're going to try,' I said. 'Remember when we were hiding in that tomb in the City of the Dead?' I feel her head move and assume she's nodding. 'Well, we were in danger then and got out. And even though this is dangerous, we'll get out of here as well.'

'Are there bad men looking for us?'

'Maybe.'

I try to remember the path I took through the tomb to get here, but of course almost all that was in darkness. I try to remember the plan of the tomb I stole, but why would that show a tunnel?

'Think,' I say out loud.

'Think,' Imi echoes.

'Best not to think,' the Quiet Gentleman says. 'Best just to do. We're going to head for the entrance.'

260

'And?'

'We'll see.'

I hear the chink of metal on metal as he lifts up his bag of tools and, with Imi hanging on to me, follow the sounds of his movement.

By keeping to the right-hand wall, it's easy enough to feel our way up the first set of steps, through the long gallery and then to the final steps that should have led us out. As we near the foot of the stairs we start to feel broken rock and picking a way through it is hard. The Quiet Gentleman goes on ahead. I hear him rummage in his tool bag and then *chink, chink, chink.*

Each blow of the chisel makes a tiny spark as metal hits rock. In the flashes of white light I see his grim face and then the rock that's been rolled into the doorway. It's huge.

'They rolled a big rock across the entrance and must have backfilled it with smaller stones,' he says. 'It'd take me a month to cut through and we'll be dead long before that.'

Imi starts to cry.

'But we'll sort something out,' I say. 'This escape tunnel. It'll be near the entrance, right?'

'Maybe.'

I feel the walls. They are rough plaster. Plaster is something I've learned about in Thutmose's workshops. 'You said they replastered over the tunnel,' I say.

'I said they probably did.'

'If it's new plaster, it'll feel different. It has to.'

I set to work, feeling the walls. From the steps to the entrance of the great hall I run my hands over every bit of them. Sometimes I think the plaster feels as if it has a different texture or is damper or drier, but when I ask the Quiet Gentleman to hack away at it with his chisel the answer is always the same. Solid rock underneath.

I slump to the floor, then jump up. The ceiling! The floor!

The Quiet Gentleman is tall enough to reach the ceiling and tap it with his mallet. Nothing sounds hollow. I take a chisel and tap it on the stone floor with the same results.

I slump again.

'I don't like the dark,' Imi says miserably. 'I want to play outside.'

Fair enough. It's more or less what the princess said to me. I think back to the time we spent on the roof. It seems like another life; it seems like another person. Was it really me that climbed down and stole the plan of the tomb? I close my eyes and try to remember it.

There was a long main bit – we've just been in that, but wasn't there a side chamber too, almost as long as the main tomb, but bent like an elbow . . .?

Suddenly I'm on my feet again because I'm not just seeing a plan of the tomb, I'm seeing the plan of the rocky valley with all its twists and turns, outcrops and gulleys.

'You said the tunnel would be near the way out so they wouldn't have to dig through too much rock.'

'Ye-es.'

'The side chamber. The first one.' I'm so excited I can hardly get the words out.

'What about it?'

'It must run along the side of the valley, but suppose there's a gulley cutting into the valley side! That would mean the . . .'

By the sound of it, the Quiet Gentleman has risen to his feet and is moving off towards the side chamber. '. . . tomb wall could be much nearer the valley side,' I finish off limply. 'Isn't that where they would put the escape tunnel?'

I take Imi's hand in mine and together we grope our way to the side chamber. I can hear the Quiet Gentleman a few paces behind us, tapping the walls.

'I'm right, aren't I?' I say.

'You might be. It's not like the tomb builders to do anything obvious, such as building their tunnel near the tomb entrance. If the gulley turns round to the left after the tomb entrance, that means this corner will be the place.'

Tip-tap. Tip-tap. The sound of his hammer. *Tip-tap. Tip-tap. Thud.*

'Here!' I follow the sound of his voice, one hand on the wall. He hits the wall again. I touch it. The plaster is smoother here and colder to the touch. I run my hands over the surrounding area and find a patch four handspans square.

I guide the Quiet Gentleman to the centre of the patch. 'There,' I say.

One blow, two blows, three blows. On the fourth, something cracks. On the fifth, stone falls. On the sixth, we feel a different sort of air blowing into the tomb and on the seventh the wall collapses and we find the tunnel loosely packed with rubble. Air from outside is blowing through it. We've done it.

55. In which we jump out of the frying pan and into the fire

Spiders. Snakes. Scorpions. I don't care. Grazed hands. Bruised knees. Bumped head. Don't care about them either. The tunnel ends behind a boulder. It's a squeeze to get through, then a squeeze to get around the boulder and then there's a scraggy thorn bush to avoid and we're out.

It's dawn. Imi's free. I'm free. The Quiet Gentleman's free. But we don't celebrate. There is something in the grey light that makes us feel wary. So we move quietly down the valley, on the lookout for guards and clues to tell us who blocked us in the tomb.

The valley is narrow and empty, but soon it will fill with

light and then we must somehow escape across the desert under the pitiless eye of the sun. We reach the head of the valley and stop.

'Does it strike you as odd,' the Quiet Gentleman says, 'that we haven't seen a single guard or any of the tomb builders? If they blocked us in, I would have thought that they'd be out looking to see what they did at first light.'

'Maybe they think their job's done,' I say.

'Maybe.'

As we leave the valley, a gentle breeze fans our faces. The Quiet Gentleman sniffs the air.

'No one's cooking breakfast.'

Imi says: 'I'm scared.'

I think it's the silence and it's beginning to get to me too.

On we walk, the sun clearing the mountains behind us. Now the walled tomb builders' town is in sight and, if anything, I begin to feel even more worried. No smoke is rising and the small settlement gives off a sense of emptiness, as if the inhabitants have just upped and left in the night.

Then we hear a scream. It rises, falls and is suddenly cut off. We stop dead in our tracks.

'I don't like the sound of that,' the Quiet Gentleman says. 'We should go back.'

'They helped us,' I say.

'We paid them.'

'I didn't,' I say. 'They helped me. I've got to go and see.'

But it's not just that they helped me. I want to find out more about them. I want to find out more about me. Because now I really want to find out whether there is someone in the town who might know about my past, someone who might know about a baby boy who was sent downriver in a basket for the crocodiles to eat.

'Please,' I say, 'look after Imi.'

And I run off. The sky is greying. Dawn is coming.

I make my way round the walls of the little town, keeping close to them all the way, but when I see what's happening I forget that I'm meant to be hiding and step out into the open.

Every man, woman and child is in front of the town, standing in ragged rows. They are being guarded by a lot of soldiers. Some are in chariots, an archer on the back of each one, arrows on the bowstring; most are standing around the builders and their families in a rough ring, their swords drawn.

I swallow. What's going on? In the dim light I can make out a small figure lying on the ground just outside the cordon of guards. Someone is sobbing. He tried to escape. The guards cut him down.

An uneven rocky outcrop hides me as I leave the protection of the walls, then I wriggle along a rainwater gulley to get as near to him as possible.

When I'm close, I stick my head up. The figure on the

ground is a boy, and in spite of the blood on his face, I recognise him as the one I met in the cave – the one who looked like me.

I'm close enough to see that he's breathing; close enough to hiss at him to attract his attention. His eyes flicker open when he hears me, then widen in surprise. I hold up a hand to show he should lie still and wriggle closer.

'Are you all right?' I whisper.

He shakes his head. 'Can you move?' I try again and try to mime crawling.

He lifts his head and winces – it must hurt – but manages to inch forward until his head is over the edge of the gulley. Then I help him down and we both crouch so we're out of sight.

'What happened?' I ask.

'Soldiers. King – he coming,' the boy says.

'Here? Why?'

The boy pulls a finger across his throat. 'You dead,' he says hoarsely. 'Last night at tomb. Soldiers. You.'

'You mean they blocked the tomb last night?' I say. 'It was them?'

'Yes! Soldiers. Tomb is big secret.'

'So secret that they want to kill everyone who has anything to do with it?'

The boy shrugs. 'King is coming.'

'When?'

'Now, maybe.'

I put my head over the edge of the gulley and look across the desert in the direction of the king's city. I see a cloud of dust, a flash of silver. The king is coming to see his tomb in his chariot of polished silver.

I look at the boy; the boy looks at me. What can I do? Walk away, back to the Quiet Gentleman and whatever he's decided he needs to do, or try to talk to the king?

In the end my mind is made up for me. I hear shouting and there's a stir on the edge of the cordon of guards. Two move at a brisk, disciplined trot towards the source of the noise and I see the Quiet Gentleman with two guards on his back and one on each arm, refusing to go down. It's the guards shouting for help, not him.

One moves away, holding a squirming bundle. It's Imi and without really thinking I'm running towards her. She sees me and holds her hands out, but I am caught before I reach her and lifted off the ground and a fist slams hard into the side of my head. I blink, but the world has blurred, then goes black and turns upside down as I'm thrown over the guard's shoulder and carried to the main body of guards.

Where we wait.

56. In which I speak

The king stands on the back of his silver chariot, looking nowhere much, and his face is completely blank. Suddenly I remember one of the rock carvings in the ruined temple by the pyramids. It showed a giant king, striding over a battlefield of slain enemies, a sword in his hand. He had his feet planted on a field of his headless victims and his face was calm.

This is part of what kings do, I think. Someone decides not to kill them and they take it as their due. They kill people and they don't mind. They are different from the rest of us.

One of the guards approaches the chariot and throws himself forward on his face. The king waits then tells him to rise.

'The builders are assembled, Your Highness,' he says. 'There were others in the tomb. Thieves.' He spits the word out. 'We brought them out.'

'A messenger told me they had been sealed inside,' the king answers. 'Why did you release them?'

'They escaped. We don't know how. There must have been a side tunnel.'

'I thought we had prevented that.'

The head guard looks miserable. 'There are always ways in, Lord. We don't know how it happened. These builders, they're foreign. They have tricks. I . . .'

'It does not matter. They must all die,' the king says. 'It is decreed.'

'But that's all wrong!' Shock rips the words out of my mouth.

The king's head swings in my direction. 'Who spoke?' he asks.

'We think he's one of the thieves,' the head guard says. 'A boy. They use them for squeezing down small holes.'

'Show me,' the king says. The guard holding me hesitates, but at a nod from his superior he holds me out in front of him at arm's length, like a lamb being shown to a butcher. I try not to bleat.

'Twice Born,' the king says. 'You are dirty.'

'My Lord, I . . .'

'Were you in my tomb?'

'It was all a mistake,' I say.

Silence. The day is brightening.

'People want to rob my tomb,' the king says. 'They imagine my death and they see a tomb full of grave goods.'

'I know. I . . .'

'They are wrong to do this.'

I don't know what to say. In among all the mystery and adventure, perhaps we have overlooked the big thing that maybe it really is wrong to rob a tomb. And yet . . . is that what the king means?

I can't really puzzle it out because he's talking again.

'Twice Born. Walk to me, stand before me and tell me that you could not do such a thing.'

Another hesitation from the guard, another hissed order.

I am put down and walk to the king. I don't throw myself on to the ground. I want to look at his face. I want to understand his expression as badly as if I am going to make it with my hands. I feel an excitement gathering inside me.

I am standing by the king's chariot now. Its silver plates are dulled with desert dust. To look up at the king, I have to crane my neck. The horses tug against their reins and snicker. The chariot creaks as it moves forward and back.

The king looks down at me.

Tell me you could not do such a thing.

Can I lie? No. Not now that it has come to this.

Tell me you could not do such a thing.

I unwind my thoughts like pictures on a scroll.

They imagine my death and they see a tomb full of grave goods. They are wrong to do this.

That is what the king just told me. Does he mean they are wrong because it's a bad thing to do? No. He didn't say that. He did not say that at all.

What happens when the king dies? He is buried with the finest grave goods. But what happens when *this* king dies?

He is buried in the sun's horizon. I remember it. I remember the notch in the mountain filling with gold. The tomb filling with gold.

A great silence holds me and then the words are in my mouth, each one a piece of gold, each one a treasure.

'Why would I try to rob an empty tomb?' I ask the king. 'Why would I try to rob a tomb that is never going to be filled with gold? The only wealth the king needs is the gold of the sun. His tomb is in the sun's horizon. Every morning the sun's horizon fills with the light of the sun. That is enough for the king. He knows this and I know this, so why would I enter the king's tomb to steal what cannot be stolen? Why would I enter the tomb to steal what will never be there?'

'And why can't it be stolen?' the king asks.

'Because the light of the sun is not to be given or taken,' I say. 'The sun just is.'

And the king smiles.

'We shall not kill Twice Born,' he says.

'Or his sister,' I say. 'Please.'

'Or his sister, if it pleases him.'

'Or these people,' I say, gesturing at the tomb builders. 'If they hadn't helped me, my sister would be buried in your tomb and would not be alive for you to save.'

'If I do not kill them,' the king says, 'then I must send them far away where they cannot tell people of my tomb or its secrets.'

'I'm sure they won't mind that,' I say.

'There is one other,' the king says. 'You have not mentioned him. My spies told me that a great criminal came to my city. That he was travelling with a boy and a girl. That he has done great harm. That he intended to do me great harm. My spies told me this because there is a reward for his capture in my great city of the north and my great cities of the south. Such a reward would make any man rich. Or any boy.'

I think. I think of the Quiet Gentleman and the trouble he brought with him. I think of the number of times I might have lost my life. I think of what he did not tell me. I think of his plan to kill the king and how I so nearly did it. Everything bad that happened to me was because of him.

But then again, did I really want my old life back, the one I had before I saw a stranger walking across the desert in a cloud of dust?

I would not have met the king. I would not have met the princess. And more importantly, I would not be who I am right now. To kill him would be to kill a bit of me.

All these thoughts while I breathe in and while I breathe out.

'Oh, him,' I say. 'He was a drunk. He fell off the boat and got eaten by crocodiles. Nasty piece of work. Deserved everything that happened to him, if you want my opinion.'

And I breathe in the king's silence.

57. In which I find my place

And breathe out again. And in. And out.

Because that's what you do. That's what you do all day long and all night too in order to stay alive and you do it without thinking. No one has the right to take that away.

Deep breath. And now for the rest.

I do not marry the princess. I do not become the king's favourite. I do not tell him that the queen is scared of growing old and he should be kind to her so she's less frightened. I do not tell him that everyone thinks his plans for the city are mad. I do none of these things because I never see him again. He rides off with an escort and the captain of the guard, who up until a minute ago was getting ready to kill us all, now has to look after us.

King's orders.

'Right,' he says. 'You heard the king. Get ready to pack up and ship out. Gather here at midday. Bring all the food and water you can.'

'But where are we going?' a grey-haired old man with a long scarf around his head asks.

'Wherever the first ship that will take you is heading. North or south. You'll be taken over the border and forbidden entry to the Two Kingdoms. Is that clear?'

His eyes glide over me, then towards the Quiet Gentleman and Imi. 'But not us,' I say. 'The king was talking about the tomb builders.'

'Not what I heard.'

'Who knows the king better than me?' I ask with complete certainty of the answer.

The captain's mouth falls down at the corners.

'Right,' he says. 'All right.'

The builders accept their fate without discussion. They file back into the walled town. Not long after, cooking fires are lit and bread is baked for the journey.

Just before midday, the first of them file out, possessions wrapped in blankets. Stretchers are made up there and then for the sick and elderly. Next officials from the city arrive on horseback in a huge hurry. There are tallymen to count heads and scribes to write it down. There's a collection of tools – every hammer and every chisel, every trowel and every spade is accounted for and laid out on the ground.

I remember what Mahu said about the glory of the Two Kingdoms being in the way everything is measured, but there's no way you can measure luck. The wonder of this place is how everything is measured and is still so strange.

Across the desert, a plume of smoke is rising from the Great Temple's fire altar. The king will be there, and the queen, and the princess, but I can't believe I was ever there. It's like a dream; it's like I was different person.

The quiet I felt when I talked to the king has somehow stayed inside me. I don't know why, but I'm close to tears a lot of the time we're walking across the desert.

Things get better on the boat that is taking us north. When the tomb builders hear my story, they immediately call me Moshe, which means Pulled From Water in their language, and try to persuade me to come with them. I'm tempted, but something else they say makes me think I should go home: how can a poor fisherman, they wonder, too poor to own a boat, go from scratching a living on the riverbank to owning an inn? Only one explanation, they say: my birth mother left money in the basket before she pushed me into the river and the man who found me spent it on the inn. The inn is mine!

That tells me there's unfinished business at home and although part of me wants to travel north and then across a desert and over a mountain to a land flowing with milk and honey, another part of me wants to sort stuff out back where it all began.

Anyway, I want to deliver Imi back home, safe and sound. I want to see her happy again.

The tomb builders take a collection to see us on our way and we leave them at the same port from which Imi, the Quiet Gentleman, Jatty and I set off on our journey south. Nothing has changed: the same forest of masts, the same bellowing cattle, the same jars of oil and grain . . . all going to the City of the Sun's Horizon. I can't explain how, but it seems as if we arrived at the port the day before yesterday, but all that happened in the city was a lifetime ago.

We hitch a ride on the back of a cart and I watch the pyramids fill more and more of the sky as we approach.

'Still think you're doing the right thing?' the Quiet Gentleman asks as we reach the outskirts of the town.

'I'm more scared than when Mahu arrested me. I'm more scared than when I talked to the king. I'm more scared than when we were walled up in his tomb.'

'That's because it's your decision to come back and not anyone else's,' he says. 'Funny that.'

'Hilarious,' I say. 'Why didn't you tell me it would be hard?'

'And ruin your fun?' he asks. 'Never.'

'What are you going to do?'

He shrugs. 'Get to the inn and see what's what. Then decide.'

'Good,' I say.

But when we get to the inn, there's a surprise. The courtyard gate is off its hinges. There are little piles of earth all over the place as if people have been digging. The roof timbers for the kitchen and the guests' sleeping quarters have been stolen so the roofs have fallen in. It's desolate.

In a cavity in a wall, I find one of my little animals, put there by Imi. When I hand it to her she looks at me, amazed. I don't think she even realises this is home.

I go to the shrine. More chaos. All the flagstones in the

floor have been lifted and smashed and sand covers the floor.

The Quiet Gentleman grabs a passer-by and asks him what happened. It appears that, shortly after we left, rumours started that the inn was sheltering tomb robbers. The townspeople broke down the door, rescued my parents and chased Nebet and Bek out of town. Then they started tearing the place apart to try and find the treasure they were sure was hidden somewhere.

'What happened to the couple who ran the place?' I ask.

I recognise the man as an occasional drinker. He blinks at me then bows.

'Why, little master, they went to the next town to stay with the woman's sister.'

It's a shock to realise he doesn't recognise me, and with my shaved head and court clothes – even court clothes I've walked across a desert in, escaped from a tomb in and worn on a boat for four days – he thinks he should look up to me.

So off I go with Imi, leaving the Quiet Gentleman at the inn. In my mind, there's going to be a scene with the innkeeper and his wife. I'm going to tell them what has happened and what I've become. I'm going to tell them that I met the queen and the king and the princess. I'm going to tell them that I know who I am now and I'm better than them; better than them in every way and they'd better agree with me or else, or else, or else . . .

Of course it's not like that. Outside the aunt's house, I see a broken old man and his broken old wife, sitting on a bench and doing nothing much except stare.

'Off you go, Imi,' I say and she knows what to do.

She screams, 'Mummy!' and runs to the old woman, who stands, the years falling off her. Her face twists into an expression that's so happy it looks like grief. 'Imi,' she cries and opens her arms to her daughter.

When Imi turns round, I will be gone. I won't want to say goodbye to her. I'll have turned round and will be walking back to the inn, maybe taking a short cut through the City of the Dead, maybe not. And maybe the Quiet Gentleman will have left the inn or maybe he will have stayed.

And if he's stayed, maybe I'll ask him to leave, or stay, or let him decide. And maybe we'll set the inn up and get it running, or maybe not.

I don't know. I don't know. I don't know. And right now, that feels like freedom, and that freedom feels like treasure and it is golden.

It is all the gold of the sun.

Also from
JAMIE BUXTON

TEMPLE BOYS

Flea is the smallest, mouthiest member of
the Temple Boys – a street gang who fight daily to
survive in a place where nobody cares a jot for them,
especially not the Romans who are in charge of the place.

When the magician comes to town, Flea and
the gang are sure they can get the better of him.
But all is not as it seems . . .

'The endearing character of Flea
shines out like a star.' DAILY MAIL

Nominated for the Carnegie Medal